Green Time

Dear Herb,

Best wishes for
a happy healthy

new year.

Enjoy

Russ

GREEN TIME
Stories

edited by

Jean Lenihan

To order additional copies of this book, contact:
Xlibris Corporation
1-888-795-4274
www.Xlibris.com
Orders@Xlibris.com
21103

Contents

GREEN TIME

14 New Stories from Seattle

Mary Bruno
Ben Gebhardt
Courtenay Gebhardt
Michelle Goodman
Jason Herman
Deborah F. Lawrence
Elizabeth McCarthy
Lisa Orlick
Lucy Pond
Mindy Schaberg
Julie Schickling
Sunny Speidel
Erika Teschke
Gloria Upper

Seattle, Washington
2003

The Good Shepherd Center in Seattle, Washington

INTRODUCTION

This collection features 14 stories written in the winter and spring of 2002 during an independent fiction-writing workshop held at one of Seattle's moodiest settings: the Good Shepherd Center in Wallingford. Formerly a girls' home run by the Sisters of the Good Shepherd, the landmark public-use center looms over a walled, overgrown 11-acre garden carved from a busy residential neighborhood. Crossing the sprawling lawns to the stone entrance steps, one senses that the Italianate palace still casts long shadows of strained, cloistered lives from decades past.

The atmospheric setting of the Good Shepherd Center ignites and lingers in the mind—which is why we've interspersed Tim Rounds' recent photographs of the center with these new works of fiction. But don't let the cool silence of these pictures fool you—both the place and our process were drafty and loud. The building itself is an echo chamber; a little noise goes a long way. During the first hour of our class time each Thursday afternoon, one of the center's cleaning volunteers ran an industrial-strength vacuum back and forth across the lobby floor for a half hour before the roar faded up the grand staircase. When spring arrived and we threw the windows open, a children's bongo class sprung up on a nearby patch of grounds. In the hallway right outside our door, a popular snack machine dropped its clunky purchases throughout the afternoon.

Yet the unsealed environment was not a problem for us. This was a group of older, wiser students who were not unfamiliar with noise, both internal and external. For the 12 weeks that we met in room 221—a main-floor meeting room with ceiling-high, heavily sashed windows and a chalky, antique smell—there was steady conviviality, dissention, and energy. It meant a lot that Lucy Pond (class pet!) was always there early to preheat the room with her frolicsome glow. Thanks too must be paid to Erika Teschke, who found the room's light switch halfway through the term.

In every season, the Good Shepherd Center grounds provide a most generous slice of green. Yet that's not the origin of this book's name, *Green Time*. The idea for the title emerged from the following exchange in Julie Schickling's story of the same name.

In the story, Green Time is the name of a Roman disco that terse, mousy Lily is dragged off to by her exuberant, pleasure-seeking roommate. Eyeing the place suspiciously, Lily asks about the name's significance as she sits marooned at a table with a young man she's just been hooked up with.

"What is 'Green Time,' anyway?" [Lily] asked. "Does it mean anything?"

"'Green Time,'" Bruce said, "it means Now. Green light. Go."

Simple, no? You give a green light and people go. That's the dream of all writing teachers, and that's what happened here in this class. Some writers penned brand new tales. Others finally finished pieces that they'd started years earlier. Jason and Courtenay pretty much wrote their stories in a single, amazing shot—blazing the way for newer writers and providing the initial foundation for this collection. Other writers went back and forth with me on edits once or twice; some worked for months, literally turning their stories inside out several times over. For whatever reason, there is an absence of gimmickry and stylistic bravado in this collection. There is a fragility that is also green.

Compiling this book was a somewhat lonely process until copyeditor Jennifer Lindsay and book designer Julie Schickling started sweating the details with me. Lisa Orlick supplied moral support when the year-old project seemed to lengthen rather than condense. And a last great generosity, artist/writer Deborah F. Lawrence created the feisty collage for this book jacket for us without charge.

We hope you enjoy this collection. We don't expect to make much money off of this book. But if we do, all proceeds of book sales will go to International PEN's Readers & Writers program.

Jean Lenihan
August 2003

Noli Me Tangere

Courtenay Gebhardt

His heart was failing. The doctor had told him this as he sat stripped to his underwear, the veins vivid in his translucent skin. Surgery was recommended, urged even, but Henri was uncertain. Already he could feel death loosening the bands— parts of him had gone free and slack, no longer subject to his control. Instinctively, he felt it would be wrong to undergo a costly surgery. He was an archbishop, not a parent or grandparent.

As Henri stepped outside into the heavy afternoon air, he tried to look at his situation objectively. Here were the people— so many people—some walking, some careening around corners on sputtering Vespas, some eating ice cream as they stood before historic monuments. So often, life was not particularly spiritual. And he, too, felt remote from death—remote, even, from his feelings about his own death.

With a wheezing gait, he passed kiosks and young couples, bypassing the streets where tourists filled the sidewalks waiting to enter the Vatican. Try as he might, he couldn't keep his mind focused on the issue. Exasperated, he turned his mind toward his next meeting, an afternoon espresso with a young priest he had befriended some years ago while lecturing in France. Mathieu was his name. He seemed to have something urgent to discuss.

Henri felt cautious around the younger man. Mathieu was the kind of radical who would eventually get himself into trouble: perhaps a rebuke from the higher ecclesia or at least an appointment in some rural area where the damage he might cause would be minimal. He began writing Henri shortly after they met, his letters effusing admiration and praise for Henri's work with the Second Vatican Council and always questioning what more "they" could do to make the Church more relevant to contemporary culture. But Henri had been more careful at his age, using the right mixture of passion and patience. His risks had always led to more offices, and he had been the youngest priest appointed bishop in the Vatican administration.

Henri reached the café and stood to recover his breath. Mirrors reflected the brassy bar and silver espresso cups above a floor dirty with hundreds of footprints. Middle-aged men lounged at the bar, talking to the bartender in their undershirts and high-waisted trousers. The archbishop glanced wearily around until he found the younger priest seated quietly in a corner, his eyes intent on an open book on the table before him.

They shook hands, and Henri couldn't help noticing that Mathieu looked more like an executive than a priest. His neck bulged slightly over the starched white collar, which his straight teeth matched precisely. He looked as if his hair had just been cut and gelled.

"Thanks for meeting with me, Father," Mathieu said earnestly.

Henri sighed and situated himself into a wicker chair that creaked with his movements. He lingered in the exchange of pleasantries, enjoying the ease of his native tongue and wishing to delay any weightier discussion. He smiled at the waitress when she came for their orders. When she left, the young priest leaned forward.

"Father," he said, "I'm glad you asked about my work. I was hoping we could discuss it."

Henri nodded for him to continue.

Mathieu cleared his throat and fixed his eyes on Henri's. "I've been working with the youth, you see. And I suppose I'm feeling a little overwhelmed."

"I think what you're feeling isn't uncommon," Henri began gently. "Pastoral care can be learned only by experience. At school you're trained in church history and doctrine—not true human incidence and interaction. Many priests feel overwhelmed when they first begin."

A pained look spread across Mathieu's face. He passed a hand over the top of his head.

"Father, it's just that sometimes I wonder if the church—I mean, we, the clergy—are doing enough to support these kids. The things they face—it's incredible." He paused to swallow and his eyes skimmed the tabletop, searching. "It's like nothing I've had to experience. Like nothing I've ever seen."

Henri spread his hands against the black of his trousers and examined the patterns of bones and veins. The young man seemed volatile, unstable. Henri felt too weak to handle him. His mind fumbled, trying to picture a group of wild Catholic youth in France. He could only conjure up his own acquaintances in the days after the war, flicking cigarettes off burned-down buildings.

"Yes, Father, I understand," was all he said.

The waitress set their espressos on the table. Mathieu took a long sip from his cup, then put it down resolutely.

"Father, I would like to tell you something—something that I haven't told anyone else. It's not about me," he said quickly, but his face flamed. "It's a young woman I helped. I—I've been wanting to tell someone, but I didn't think any of the other clergy would understand. I thought if I could share with you, you would see—"

"Trust the Church," the archbishop interrupted. The words startled them both and seemed to hang in the air between them. Henri tried to smile tenderly and he put a hand over the other man's, which he patted, beating out the rhythm of his words. "Trust the Church. Trust always to the Church. At first she may seem old and stupid, like parents do to a teenager. But in time, you'll see: she has been through it. There's nothing she hasn't seen. Nothing." And he wagged a finger as if in warning.

The younger priest bowed his head and breathed deeply. He looked as if he were retrieving his words, winding his secret back into himself. Then he looked up, his brown eyes sad and his mouth grim.

"I'm sure you're right, Father. It was silly of me to think there's anything new under the sun."

Now Henri lifted the muscles of his face and held the younger man's wrist, feeling the bone of it in his grip. He gave it an awkward shake before he released it. Then he threw back his espresso and placed his cup carefully on the saucer. He was pleased that the discussion had come—of its own accord, it seemed—to an end.

"You wrote me such wonderful letters from L'Ecole Biblique," he said. "I hope I'll receive reports on your new adventures as well." He stood and bent over the priest and kissed him on each cheek. Then he turned to go.

Outside the sun slanted so that a golden light lit up the magazine kiosks and the faces of the people who wandered aimlessly through the piazzas. As he plodded around them,

Henri considered the young priest's emotionalism. He felt irritated by it. Irritated by the way the man reflected his own youth, but with none of his political savoire faire. Henri had always had a mixed relationship with his own uncanny abilities—had used it for good, or otherwise tried to ignore it. These days, he decided, he wanted nothing to do with young rabble-rousers. Give him his glass of port, an afternoon nap, and a good meal, and he was content. But when he thought this way, he felt a mixture of anger and surprise at himself. He imagined himself dying, and he was afraid.

He pushed open the heavy door to the Church of San Severus and stepped into the dim cool. Early on in his days in Rome, Henri had discovered a series of medieval paintings in the transept of the cathedral. The small panels were dominated by thick, gilded frames whose scrollwork defied the simple geometry of the artist's lines. The work itself was neither remarkable nor famous. Yet something about the way the artist had utilized conventional beauty in some places and deliberately left it off in others conveyed a kind of purposeful meditation. It elicited in Henri an odd feeling of kinship with the anonymous artist. He would let him guide his thoughts—like some kind of patron saint, Henri felt—and soon it became a sort of language for prayer, lifting him beyond his circumstances. Then he could go on.

Today the Madonna stared back at him through her hollowed-out eyes. For the first time it looked more like a skull than a face, and he couldn't get past the image. Her hand laid limply on the overlong child. The Saviour of the World looked grotesque, his head turned straight toward the viewer while his body hugged the mother. Henri moved on. Here was Christ crucified. He closed his eyes before he looked, remembering the long, sinuous arms and legs, knobby knees, quiet peaceful face. Christ's chest seemed out of proportion in this one, and Henri had imagined once that it was because his heart was too large, breaking for love of the world. Henri whispered a feeble prayer or something more like a grunt, having to do with an instinct that told him Christ's death didn't really make a difference to the world—not even in the matter of his own death. Then he opened his eyes. Christ's mouth looked pinched, red and fleshy, but his body glowed a ghastly shade of green. It looked as if the sun were setting far, far behind him— as if it were cool around him—although the picture showed no depth. Henri couldn't recall noticing the colors before.

He left the alcove and lowered himself onto a pew. He knew the last painting as well as the others and it never struck him as deeply. *Noli Me Tangere*—"Don't hang onto me." When he found himself empty and tempted to think about how his life would have been different if he had married, he thought of Christ in this painting, admonishing Mary Magdalene. It reminded him that he had important work to do. He didn't have the energy to look at it today.

He stared vacantly at the large, thickly spined ceiling.

"Father," he whispered. It was the only plea he could muster. He longed for the Eucharist—dry bread and bitter grapes that tasted like ancient church walls. It supplied reality to the faith that eluded him.

Henri hadn't noticed the young woman who came in shortly after him. Now she walked by and took a seat in the pew in front of him. She had a tiny infant, maybe two months old, who slept soundly in a stroller that she swung to face her row. She knelt down and placed ten exquisite fingertips on the pew in front of her. She cocked her head as if to pray but her shoulders were rigid, as if she were merely concentrating. She remained that way for some time. Henri felt tender towards her—so lifelike with her creamy neck covered with a delicate lace of brown curls that had slipped from her bun. He wondered if she were a tourist and where she came from. She seemed homesick or distressed. When she sat back in her pew, he thought of ways to address her.

"Have you been to this church before?" he asked in Italian.

She turned around, surprised. "Excuse me?" she said in English.

He repeated the question in English, and she laughed and laid an arm along the back of her pew. "Oh yes. I try to come whenever I can."

"Ah," he said. "You live in Rome."

"Yeah," she said lightly, and seemed to leave it at that.

"And you are American," he said, unwilling to let her alone, to be let alone.

"Yes, from Kansas, of all places. My husband works in finance, and he got shipped over here for a few years."

Henri mused. She looked young, perhaps in her early twenties. He wondered if she had ever been away from her family before.

"How is your parish at home?" he asked at length. He couldn't quite place all of this—dim lights, old pictures, the sacraments—in Kansas. He always thought of New York. At the Vatican he had met plenty of officials from the big cities in America.

"Oh," she chuckled. "I'm Baptist. But I like it in here. It makes me feel . . . small."

"Yes," he said. "I think we all come for that." He liked her. He liked her easy manner. She had been troubled, and now it all seemed to have drifted away.

The baby began to cry, a small balled-up sound.

"Excuse me," the woman said, and plucked the child up out of the stroller. She threw a blanket over her shoulder and fumbled with her clothing before turning back slightly to face the old man. The baby hushed.

"I hope you don't mind," she said with a shy grin.

"Not at all." But the archbishop fiddled with his cuff. They remained silent for a moment, which was awkward, as she nearly faced him.

"I came to look at some paintings . . ." he began. "They're paintings that I often looked at when I was young."

She nodded.

"As you mentioned, they make me feel 'small,' you could say."

She glanced around. "Which ones?"

He pointed at the alcove to the left and behind him, but did not turn to see it himself. It felt like a great, black vacuum at his shoulder; he could feel the panels swathed in shadow.

"I can't quite make them out from here," she said, "but I'll have to have a look after this."

"Yes," he said.

He heard a sucking sound as she adjusted the baby at her breast. It let out a cry and beat at the blanket so that it fell off her shoulder. She fiddled hastily with her shirt and threw the blanket over her other side.

"She's pretty fussy," she said. Now she turned to face him the other way.

"Are you visiting, or are you kind of stationed here?" she asked.

"Yes. Stationed here. I work," he waved vaguely, "at the Vatican."

"Where are you from?"

"France," he said. Strangely, the word reminded him of the slightly vinegar scent of his childhood home in Lyons. It conjured up a picture that he hadn't thought of in years: his mother making supper, moving quickly from counter to counter, chattering to his grandmother as she chopped vegetables, boiled water, kneaded dough. He had been afraid of grandmère. He was only four when she moved in. She had no memory—had forgotten how to speak. In the kitchen her thin body would lie limp in a chair, draped in a freshly ironed pinafore, a bowl of uncut vegetables in its lap. Now and again she would lift a long finger to gesture and chuckle, as if she meant to help, as if she were trying to be hospitable.

Henri found himself staring at the young woman's mouth. "I thought so," she was saying. "I mean, you don't seem Italian." Her speech was consoling, anchoring him in the present with its lilting sounds.

"No," he said, his voice faraway. "No, but I've been here a long time."

She nodded, curious and sympathetic. "How long have you been here?"

He forced himself out of the reverie and concentrated on her question. "Oh . . . thirty, forty years, perhaps."

The baby let out another muffled cry.

"Oh, girl," the woman said, yanking off the blanket. "What's the problem?" She held the little one with her palms and forearms in front of her. All at once Henri saw the opal luster of the inside of her arms, the child's dark, staring gaze, the oversized, puckered nipple that spread across a heavy round breast. He stared in spite of himself, intent on the sudden intimacy he saw between the mother and child, so different from the baby in the painting whose gaze looked miserably outward. His grandmother, his mother, this woman, her daughter—they all seemed to collide in his mind—they all seemed to connect. He felt outside of it, a boy alone, hiding out beneath the dining room table as the chatter swept overhead, swept on without him. He felt overwhelmed with an inexpressible sorrow, feeling, somehow, that his life had been meaningless, without impact. He wanted to weep.

"Well," the woman said, suddenly aware of her bared flesh and the old archbishop. She fidgeted momentarily with her blouse and stood up with one hand supporting the baby's head against her shoulder. "I'd like to take a look at those paintings. Will you show me?"

He helped her move the stroller out of the way and followed her to the transept. They stopped at the first one and he pointed at the mother and child.

"That one. It reminds me of how Mary had to give up her most treasured thing for the world." He felt embarrassed as soon as he said it, as if he had implied that the young mother should be ashamed for doing less. He moved on quickly, almost abruptly.

"That one. It reminds me that 'God loved the world.' Do you know that Scripture?"

She nodded, but everything he said sounded hollow to him.

"That one," now he pointed at Jesus disentangling himself from Mary's grasp. He looked at Mary Magdalene, her hair in disarray, her face tearstained, but smiling, her small hands caressing his feet—the feet she had anointed. Henri paused, his finger suspended in the air. "Eh," he said.

The young woman looked at him and then back at the painting. She shifted the baby to her other shoulder and leaned forward.

"*Noli Me Tangere*," she said. "She looks desperate. Like she doesn't know if this time's the last." She stepped back slightly. "Like she would die if it were the last."

"Huh," she said, after a moment.

"I was thinking," said the archbishop, quietly, "she must be so happy to touch him again."

The young mother gazed at him for a moment while he stood there, transfixed. She reached out and tugged a bit of his black sleeve with her free hand.

"That's wonderful," she said. "Thank you."

Then she turned and went to lay her baby in the stroller. They exchanged goodbyes, and she left through the heavy door.

Henri returned to his pew, his shoulders sagging. He laid his hands on the hard oak of the seat. For the first time since his vows, he was struck by what an ordinary man he was. Not a priest longing to be a layman. But a man, with problems. Somehow he had come to feel immune to this sensation over the years. He ran a finger along the edge of the pew, pressing hard against the grain.

He wanted desperately to talk to someone—to tell how lonely all these years had been, how he knew he was dying. He thought of the young priest and was filled with a vague sense of horror. He tried to remember their words, what it was Mathieu had begun to say, but he could only trace impressions of cups clinking against saucers and the men at the bar arguing over the latest football game. He knew he had been numb and indifferent, treating the priest's intimacy like so many crumbs to be flicked off his blacks. He stood to go. He must call the man before he left Rome. He hoped he would come for a glass of port.

When Henri stepped outside, the cool air swirled around his skin. It felt soft and inviting, filled, it seemed, with the promise of forgiveness. The sky had turned a glorious haze of pink and violet, offset by the lights that now glowed in the cafés and restaurants. The streets were noisier—an occasional voice shouted or laughed above the din. Henri felt all of this, noted joyfully that he was a part of it all: a priest in his blacks, adorning the Italian scene. He passed a sidewalk gelato stand, its buckets full of freshly whipped flavors topped with almond and chocolate shavings. With his hands in his pockets, Henri lingered for a while, imagining the different tastes on his tongue before purchasing a large cup of coconut. The vendor took his money and smiled.

"Coconut is like a vacation," he said.

Henri patted him on the back. "That's right," said he, "so you and I both should eat a cup, God knows!"

He raised a large spoonful as a toast then plunged it into his mouth. The coolness made his teeth hurt, but he turned around to survey the street and celebrate.

Then, suddenly, there was a strange lull, a rich, color-filled pause. An explosion. Shots were fired; bullets pelted him like stones thrown at the wrong victim, rocking his shoulders, sending his cup spinning into the air, knocking him back onto his fragile bones.

It was crossfire, they said later, a missed target.

More than the shots, the pigeons seemed to explode—it was what everyone remembered—pigeon's wings in their faces, pigeons like great billows of smoke filling the sky—the five cracks seemed quiet as handclaps in the commotion. But when the birds left, the people saw the vendor stooped over the archbishop's body, stuttering Hail Marys and lightly touching the father's hair. The old man lay peacefully on his side, his hands curled into fists against his face, his long legs folded gently at the knee, his feet balanced one on top of the other. As the blood seeped from the tender body, reaching around cobblestones toward them, the strangers wept and clung to each other, and their grief was something like worship.

WONDER WOMAN AND SPIDER-MAN

Mindy Schaberg

Jill Hanson thought that the rock tumbler was okay, but not the miracle Darren Newman thought it was. Darren had just dumped a freshly tumbled batch into his hand and held one up reverentially.

"You put ordinary, everyday rocks in and look what comes out," he said. A pocket of amber glowed in the slanting sunlight coming through the garage door. Jill took it from him and turned it over in her hand. She shook her short brown hair out of her eyes. The amber was nice, but it wasn't *great* like a new model horse or something. "You could make your mom a necklace with this one," she suggested.

"Maybe," he said. He rested his hand on his pudgy belly as he poked through the stones.

Jill thought Darren looked kind of like a leprechaun. He wasn't small, but he had pointy ears, a round face, blond hair, and hazel eyes that looked a lot like the greenish rock he was holding. He always seemed to be looking for something magic to transform things into gold. None of the rocks looked like her eyes, which were big and brown and—her mother said—soaked up everything.

"One of these days I'm going to pick up a gem by mistake," Darren said in his know-it-all tone, each word distinctly pronounced. "It'll look like all the other rocks, but then when I open up the tumbler, it'll be a sparkling ruby and I can sell it for a thousand dollars."

"You don't just pick up rubies off the ground," Jill said.

"Yes, you can. Some places you can. My dad's going to take me to some place in the mountains where there's a ruby mine." His eyes glowed with anticipation.

"What if you were walking along kicking gravel, but really you were kicking rubies!" Jill hooted. Darren giggled.

She put the stone back in his hand. "Well, I gotta go. See ya later."

Jill jumped up the little incline to her yard, dodging the scratchy spirea bush. Through the screen door, she heard her father telling her mother about his day at the bank. Dinner sizzled on the stove. She wandered into the side yard. Even though it was just around the corner from the front door, it felt more deserted than the furthest corner of the backyard. The firewood was stacked there, but otherwise it was just a way to get from the front yard to the back without going through the house.

Jill picked up a stick and poked idly in the holes between the logs. She could hear Darren singing to himself in his garage. This would be a good place to collect sticks next time she played Pioneer Orphans with the neighborhood kids. She had invented the game where they pretended they were orphans in the wilderness and had to live on blue spruce pinecones and milkweed.

At the sound of car doors closing, she looked across the street to see Tom and his mother returning from errands. That morning she and Tom had practiced falling down her stairs like movie stuntmen. Tom was nothing like Darren. He was crazy. He knew how to swallow air and burp loudly on command. He said a cherry bomb could blow up the world, and he had one. For weeks she'd lain awake worrying about the cherry bomb, but nothing had come of it.

Tom and Darren rarely played together. Darren was polite, fastidious, and bookish. He wouldn't say "hate," like "I hate broccoli." He said, "I don't care for broccoli." He collected pictures of Shaun Cassidy from *Teen Beat*, not Lynn Swann and Terry Bradshaw from *Sports Illustrated* like she and Tom did. Once she had climbed up the cottonwood tree between their yards and gotten stuck. She remembered Darren's worried face looking up at her. "Oh, you poor thing!" he wailed. And then there was that time they'd persuaded him to join a neighborhood game of baseball, and the ball smacked into Darren's glove as he put his hands up and turned his face away. By some miracle, the ball was in his mitt, and Tom was running to second.

"Get him!" Jill screamed.

"This is preposterous!" Darren yelled, making the vain run to second where Tom was already safe.

But Darren was a good student and she was, too. They both liked to read. He was most fun when it was just the two of them.

Jill dropped the stick and dared herself to restack some of the firewood. Spiders lived among the logs, maybe even black widows and brown recluses. She'd seen black widows a couple of times around the pipes in the basement or in forgotten corners of the yard like this one. A shiver skittered down her spine. At least black widows were easy to identify, glossy black with the blood red hourglass on the underside of the swollen belly. But brown recluses looked like most other spiders: brown, nondescript, but with the telltale violin shape on the back. She picked up each piece of wood and examined it carefully.

She heard Mr. Newman's old blue truck pull into the alley. He was home from his job at the tool-making shop. The back gate clicked closed and footsteps crunched over gravel.

"What's this doing here?" Mr. Newman's voice ricocheted off the cement walls. "I told you to take out the trash when I left!"

"I was just going to!" Darren's voice was shrill.

"I was just going to," Mr. Newman mimicked. She heard a scuffle.

"Don't, dad!" Darren cried. There was a clattering sound: Darren's stones hitting the ground.

Jill heard Mrs. Newman's voice, muffled behind the screen door. "Jerry, let him go," she pleaded.

"You're going to defend this little pansy?" A heavy footstep fell.

"Dad, stop!" Darren cried.

A thud and a yelp. "You hear me? Huh? Little mama's boy."

"Jerry, stop it!"

A scuffle, and then the door slammed, and the noise faded into the house.

Jill stared at the red, twined slats of the fence. She strained her ears, but she couldn't hear anything more from the Newman's house. She sat by the woodpile, a log forgotten in her hand. She never knew Mr. Newman could be like that! She looked down at the log, dropped it like a lit match, and ran in her house.

"There you are." Mrs. Hanson smiled at Jill as she tossed the salad. "Just in time to set the table."

Jill sat at the kitchen counter and stared out at the street. She heard the rustle of the newspaper as her father turned the page in the living room.

"Did you hear me?"

"Okay." Jill got up and cleared the mail off the table.

Jill rang Darren's doorbell. He answered, his finger keeping his place in a Hardy Boys book. He didn't look any different. No bruises, no puffy eyes from crying, no arm in a sling.

"Can you play?" she asked.

"Okay," he said, opening the door for her to come in. He put down his book on the coffee table and picked up a magazine. "Look at this," he said. It was called *Nudists Like Us.*

"Is it a dirty magazine?" asked Jill, eyeing the naked, aging hippie on the cover. Tom had a stash of dirty magazines that he kept in the glove compartment of an abandoned pickup.

"It's nudism. My dad says the human body is a beautiful thing." He turned the pages.

"Is this yours?"

"No, it's his."

She examined the ordinary people like the ones she saw at the grocery store. So that was what was under all those clothes. Hair in strange places and things hanging limply. Stocky bodies, bony bodies, pear shapes, and beer bellies. Scars and dimples. One breast hanging down farther than the other. A knobby thing peeking out of a huge mound of hair. They weren't beautiful to her, they were disturbing.

"Do you want to play Superheroes?" she asked, pushing the magazine away.

"Okay." They clunked down the stairs to his basement.

"Who do you want to be?"

"I'll be Wonder Woman," said Darren. "Who do you want to be?"

"I'll be Spider-Man," said Jill as she surveyed the possibilities of the Newman's basement. It was concrete and sparsely furnished. Jill's basement had wood paneling and shag carpet. Her room was down there, and also the storage room which was her playroom. Darren's basement had an old couch with an ugly afghan over it. Still, there was lots of room to play.

"Who's going to be the bad guy first?" Darren asked.

"I will. I'll be a bank robber."

"Okay."

"So you go over there." She pointed and Darren went into the next room.

"This is a stickup. Give me all your money!" said the bank robber.

"Help, help!" said a teller.

"I hear screams!" said Wonder Woman. "They're coming from over there. Hey! You! Stop!" Darren stepped into the room and struck the classic Wonder Woman pose, hands on hips, feet planted shoulder-width apart, an imperious expression on his face.

"Oh no! Wonder Woman!" The bank robber ducked behind the couch and leveled her gun at Wonder Woman's heart, "Pow! Pow!"

Wonder Woman deflected the bullets with his golden wristbands, then twirled something above his head. "You've just been lassoed by my Golden Lasso of Truth!"

"No, I haven't."

"Yes, you have."

"How come I can't feel anything?"

"'Cuz it's magic. Try and run." Wonder Woman jerked the lasso.

The robber did a spectacular shoulder roll onto the couch.

Wonder Woman stalked over and bent down to handcuff the robber. His lips were pursed in righteous indignation. "You've just robbed the wrong bank, mister!" he hissed.

The Newmans had moved in next door two years ago. That first summer, Jill, Darren, and his younger sister, Darla, played tag on the Newman's front lawn. It was one of those endless Colorado evenings when school had just let out and the whole summer stretched ahead. The grass was green and thick underfoot, but lumpy from clods of dirt or rocks under the surface. The sun slanted through the clouds, tingeing them pale lemon and peach as it descended behind the mountains. Across the street, the bluff rose tawny and sphinx-like, its rock face bathed in the golden evening sun.

Darren rushed toward Jill with his arms wide open. He hugged her to him like a life jacket and kissed her cheek.

"Don't," said Jill. She extricated herself and ran to the edge of the grass, and hung there warily, swaying like a tennis player ready for the serve, waiting for him to commit himself so she could run the other way.

Today Jill was an eagle. She perched on top of the jungle gym and vigilantly scanned the horizon. She'd just finished building a nest with fitzer boughs. The mountains stretched as far she could see, a huge green dragon slumbering on the plains. Her eye followed along the prickly green body to a big pink gash in its side, where a granite quarry scooped out gravel for asphalt.

Mrs. Newman and Mrs. Hanson chatted over the back fence. They were talking about music lessons. Mrs. Newman had a broad, somewhat vacant face. She was always smiling and nodding, and when she spoke she sounded like she was reading from a bad script that included lots of platitudes like "Waste not, want not!" and "The Lord will provide." Her laugh was beautiful though, high and tinkly like glasses clinking.

Jill jumped down, spread her wings, and wheeled over the grass, looking for prey. The sun was warm on her back and the breeze whispered through her hair, carrying the spicy scent of cottonwood sap and the sting of juniper. She was high above the earth, floating and free. She heard Mrs. Newman's voice drop and watched her mother lean in. She circled closer.

Snippets of phrases wafted up to her: "Darren doesn't take viola anymore. He decided it was an unnecessary expense . . . Very tight-fisted with money . . . Jerry would rather I stay home instead of going to the nurses' convention . . . Well, he says it's very important to stick to a budget."

Suddenly, Mrs. Newman jumped and looked at her watch. "Oh, I have to get the clothes out of the dryer. Jerry doesn't like me to use the dryer. He prefers for me to use the clothesline." She disappeared into the garage.

"Look at my nest, Mom!" Jill shouted as Mrs. Hanson turned away from the fence.

"Beautiful," said her mother, and pulled a weed out of the garden.

That night as she lay in bed, Jill saw Mr. Newman's face like an angry bulldog looming up in the dark. Tight-fisted. Mrs. Newman's soft voice and high, tinkly laugh. Rocks clattering on the cement floor. Darren's strangled, high yelp of pain. Tight-fisted.

She turned over. Her dad spanked her when she was bad, like the time she'd thrown mud balls at his homing pigeons, but she knew it was coming and could prepare herself for it. He'd gotten so mad once when she was in second grade that he knocked things off the counter. She didn't know what had made him that mad, but it wasn't her forgetting to do a chore.

Tom didn't have a dad. He'd left the family after Tom's little sister was born. He worked in a funeral home, embalming people. Who would want to do that? Tom was getting bossy with his mom. If he wanted to ask her something and she was vacuuming, he'd just turn off the vacuum! Jill thought that was rude, but his mother didn't seem to mind. Now he was kind of hanging out with some bad kids.

Sometimes Mr. Newman was nice to the neighborhood kids. He showed Jill how to tie a slip knot when she was practicing lassoing a garbage can, and he told Tom how to pitch a knuckle ball, though he couldn't actually demonstrate it because of his leg. He had been a Marine in Vietnam, or maybe Korea, and had an old leg injury. (Darren's sister Darla had told her that. Darla was the apple of Mr. Newman's eye. He liked to call her "Sister.") So he never wore shorts, not even when it was ninety degrees. He kept the scar and shrapnel or whatever it was deeply hidden.

Jill and Darren rode their bikes up and down their street. Jill liked to pretend they were horseracing, crouched over the handlebars, legs bumping against their bellies, other times drag racing, leaning back in the seat, refueling at the lilac bush by her driveway. But mostly they just chatted, coasting down the street almost to the light, watching to make sure a car wasn't speeding around the curve. Then they circled back, pedaling up the other side of the street to the flat end where they lived.

Today Darren recited the latest big words he had memorized, "Oscillate, to swing back and forth, to waver," but Jill wasn't listening. She was thinking about what she had heard Mrs. Newman say. She dropped back and watched Darren riding his bike with the banana seat and the high handlebars. She watched the road blur under her tires. She knew she wasn't supposed to tell Darren what she had heard, but why shouldn't he know? *I shouldn't tell him, but I want to tell him. I shouldn't tell him, but I want to tell him,* her brain chanted, waiting for a sign to keep or spill its secret. *I shouldn't, I shouldn't, I shouldn't.*

Darren paused in his recitation. In the silence, she felt the secret brimming over into her mouth. She pumped to catch up.

"Do you know what your mom told my mom?" she asked, pulling even.

"No, what?"

"She said your dad was very tight-fisted."

"What?"

"She said he made you give up your viola lessons because they were too expensive."

"When did she say that?"

"I don't know, she told my mom."

"She said he was parsimonious?"

"What's that?"

"Stingy."

"Well, she said he wouldn't let her go to her nurses' conference."

Darren pedaled in silence.

Jill skidded to a stop where a gravel cul de sac met the road. "Do you think they'll get a divorce?"

Darren slowed to a stop. "No," he said thoughtfully.

"Why not?"

"I don't think that's true," he said.

"Why would she tell my mom?"

"I don't know."

Jill pried a pebble out of her tire tread and tossed it away. Darren watched it fall and carefully picked it up. He put it in his pocket and got on his bike. "So what did she say again?"

Jill repeated what she had heard.

Jill was reading the Sunday comics on the couch in the living room when the phone rang. Her mother answered, "Hello . . . Oh, hello, Mary." Jill pricked up her ears.

"No, not that I'm aware of, why?" She was quiet a long time. "Oh, Mary, I'm so sorry."

She hung up and stood with her hand on the phone. The hair on Jill's arms stood up. She tried to brush it down again. Her mother's voice crackled like lightning. Had she told Darren something she'd overheard? Jill peeked at her mother's ashen face. Her eyes made Jill drop her gaze quickly. She'd never seen her mother's eyes look like that.

Mrs. Hanson towered over her daughter. "Darren didn't want to go to Sunday school this morning, so he told his father something Mrs. Newman told me. How did he find out?"

The answer yawned like a black hole in front of them.

"Don't make it worse by lying, Jill."

Jill stared darkly at the *Prince Valiant* comic. The color was splotched over. The red of his lips was on his ear. "I told," she said quietly.

"Oh, Jill." Mrs. Hanson sat down. "Sometimes you don't want anyone else to know what you tell someone. Like a secret. Darren did a very hurtful thing. And you did, too."

Jill stared at the carpet.

"Well, Darren's grounded for a month," said Mrs. Hanson, standing up. "And you, young lady, are grounded for a week."

She watched her mother disappear into the bedroom.

"Well, there goes that friendship," she heard her mother say to her father as the door closed. "Poor Mary burst into tears."

Jill went outside. She peered through the slats of the Newman's fence. Their house was as quiet as a tomb. The pit of her stomach felt like it was filled with rocks. She squatted as if pulled down by the awful weight and idly picked blades of grass.

A door squeaked and Darren wandered into his backyard. His face was blotchy, like he'd been crying, but he had a strange new defiant air about him. He plopped in a lawn chair and began flipping through a catalog.

"Psst, Darren!"

He looked over. His eyes lit up briefly and then returned to opaque flatness.

"I heard what happened," she whispered. "You're grounded for a month!"

"Yeah," whispered Darren, "and we're not going to the ruby mine, either. He said I didn't even deserve to go to a gravel pit." He sounded nonchalant.

"Oh," Jill hung miserably on the slats of the fence.

He shrugged and turned the page of the catalog. "Look. I'm saving my allowance to get one of these."

Jill looked where he pointed. It was picture of a metal detector. The caption read: *Find buried treasure in your own backyard!*

THE MESSENGER

Lisa Orlick

Spring is fluid and confusing this year. Warm desert breezes move freely and unencumbered. Yet the summer heat has arrived early. It's only May and already the thick warmth has returned. And today, for certain, Yaacov Spletzmann—postmaster emeritus, child survivor of Buchenwald—should deliver the annual parcel from America. Since 1974, Yaacov has handled with great care the parcel from Aliza Adino. He doesn't fold it, bend it, or crush it into the small mailbox. He'll hand the parcel to Aaron, as he has done each and every year.

Yaacov walks the streets of Rehavia, along the narrow slabs of cement undulating with the contours of the Jerusalem hills, while Aaron paces his apartment, sliding his bare feet against the cool stone floor, looking at the clock, folding and unfolding the newspaper, shaking the coins in his pants pockets. The palms of his hands slide around the back of his neck; then he places them under the waist of his pants, filling the curve of his lower back. Restless and impatient, Aaron wanders into the garden. Here he can sit at the table surrounded by flower pots and vines climbing the walls. As he rubs his hands together, there is the sound of sandpaper on freshly cut wood. He waits.

Yaacov's delivery route includes many of the oldest buildings in the West Jerusalem neighborhood. For over fifty years, the same families have lived here. After World War I, in the early 1920s, the Greek Orthodox Church sold off hundreds of *dunams*. Then Rehavia was just a rock-strewn, thorny hillside. Quiet. Wild land. There was only the Ratisbonne Monastery to the north and the old windmill to the southeast. The land was deserted and useless.

Yaacov walks beneath the linens that hang from clotheslines laced between kitchen windows. White sheets. White towels. Undergarments and shirts. All bleached. A silent, dolorous white. A fresh white linen tablecloth ready to be smoothed across the Sabbath dining table. The clean cotton shirts a mother washed for a child. And the memory of the dead, buried without cotton shrouds in his concentration camp. Yaacov quickens his step. Aaron is waiting. He knows what waiting did to his soul.

At 18 Rav Berlin Street, Aaron and Miriam HaLev are one of eight families still living in the four-story walkup. No one has moved from here in 40 years. No one, that is, except Aliza and Michael Adino. Aliza is the one who planted the crest of *hatzav* that meanders along the walkway to the apartment building, pushing green leaves to conceal the sandy soil. Every spring the foliage is a tease that unexpectedly dies off at the peak of the season. No flowers. No intoxicating fragrance. Yet in autumn the saplings return with abundant white flowers.

Aaron and Miriam's neighbors have lived under the same roof for countless years. They are a constant presence in each other's lives. They never share intimate details. They just allow each other to observe and to know what is happening, without revealing the whole story.

"*Erev tov*, Aaron. Is Miriam back to work yet?" Mrs. Uttermann will ask as she clips a few garden flowers for her dinner table. "We saw your pictures from Shoshanna Guttmann's wedding. Her mother was so pleased." Mrs. Uttermann's thin red lips curl with the compliment. "How did you get Sara's good side for the family picture? A master. You are a master, Aaron."

"*Boker tov*, Aaron. *Gut morgen*." Every morning Mr. Hoffman greets Aaron as they search the walkway for their morning newspapers. "Today they say rain. What do you think?"

"Not a chance, Mr. Hoffman." Aaron smiles and plays along with Mr. Hoffman's simple sense of humor as he unfurls his newspaper.

From the communal garden, Aaron can hear the Charniaks' dinner conversations next door, Avital singing Russian lullabies to her daughter before nightfall, and the clatter of cutlery against the porcelain dishes at the Hoffmans' apartment on the third floor. On Thursday evenings, Aaron anticipates wafts of late-baking challah that the evening breeze brings to his open windows. Sweet challah. The braided egg bread replete with golden raisins at the Hoffmans. Mrs. Charniak bakes her challah with chocolate chips for her grandchildren.

Miriam and Aaron are often lulled into slumber with Amalia Uttermann's late-night concertos in apartment 1B. She is a private instructor for the best students in the neighborhood. They come to her from all over the city, from as far off as Tel Aviv. Two young boys from East Jerusalem and even children from the Arab village of Beit Tzafafa come once a week.

When it's eight o'clock, dusk, with pink skies and evening breezes, the students are still running up the stairwell for a late master-level class with their teacher. School bags banging against the railing. Sandals slapping against the stone steps. Aaron is undisturbed by these comings and goings. When he is desperate for the largeness of life in Jerusalem to disappear, he invites these sweet evenings to delude him and consume him with a false sense of security.

"Absurd," Aaron mutters. He has wandered out to the garden to look out for Yaacov. Miriam has risen to prepare their breakfast. Tea, toast, a plate of soft cheese, tomatoes, onions, and cucumbers sliced thin and plentiful. "Absurd, Miriam. No one sends letters anymore; just irrelevant mail." He is still folding and refolding the morning newspaper. He hasn't read it. He can only imagine a perfect envelope, a letter. Even a postcard would suffice.

"There's e-mail, Aaron, cell phones, instant communication. You like that, don't you?" The corners of Miriam's mouth deepen with a smile of refrained satisfaction. She knows Aaron is complaining so as to distract himself from his waiting. She knows Aaron is addicted to his e-mail. For that reason, the conversation is delightful for her. Aaron is acting like a teenager, protesting that public transportation is superior after failing his driving test. He reads newspapers on the Internet, visits eBay at least once a week to search for used camera equipment, checks how many hits there are on his wedding website. She knows it really isn't written missives he pines for; he wants the parcel from Aliza.

Miriam comes through the doorway. She sits down at the white Formica table in the garden to eat with her husband. They're lucky to have access to the garden from their kitchen. Mrs. Hoffman doesn't hide her jealousy. Miriam reaches for the newspaper sitting neatly folded under Aaron's place mat.

"I wish you had a cell phone, Miriam." Now that she's reminded him of his love for technology, he can't resist gently teasing her about the phone. "I think you're the only one in the entire country who doesn't beep and ring in public places."

"You know I hate cell phones," Miriam replies. "I hate how I have to listen to people talk about their personal lives, so loud at the bus stop, between aisles in the Supersol Market, even sitting on Ben Yehuda Street. Okay, Ben Yehuda, I can live with, you're supposed to socialize there. But what about sitting with friends at a café, talking to them, face to face, *and* another simultaneous conversation on the cell phone, all at the same time? That's too much for me." She spreads the soft cheese on her bread and covers it with thin slices of tomato and cucumber. She shakes her head in disbelief. "Every small and insignificant detail of their day, he said . . . she said . . . you said what? Who said what?" Miriam is clearly imitating her sister, Rachel, with her cell phone constantly ringing. They both laugh and pause. "Besides if everyone else has one of those damn things, it is unlikely I won't be able to make a call of necessity, right?"

"Right, Miriam. Of course you are right. You'll always be able to grab a phone from a stranger and say, 'It's a call of necessity, give me your phone, now!'" They laugh. The air is so warm. Aaron is dreaming again about the mail and the letters he misses. He misses sealing an envelope with a single wet lick. He misses stamps. He misses the anticipation.

Aaron has saved handwritten copies of all the love letters he wrote to Miriam. Letters from the army. Letters from when he was in New York apprenticing with a photographer. Often he has wondered if she would be embarrassed to find the shoebox in the back of the cedar closet in their bedroom. He likes to imagine her cheeks flushing to discover the box full of his writings. And the old snapshots. At that time his only camera was a used Brownie. Black-and-whites the size of baseball cards with scalloped edges and a date scribbled on the back of each photo. There she is, looking to see if anyone is in the room, and then, when she is sure she is alone, he can picture her nestled in bed with the entire box's contents. He likes to think she'd read each letter searching for a new secret to uncover. He imagines a mosaic of photos covering her legs; photos of her with friends at a party, eyes bright and laughing, bodies embracing, and images of her sleeping on the beach in Sinai, her skin dark, naked shoulders, and sun-bleached hair.

It is the second week in May. Independence Day is next week. It will be the anniversary of Aliza's daughter's death. If Yaacov doesn't deliver the parcel today, there are only three more deliveries before the anniversary. Aaron's impatience is more desperate this year. It's not just the parcel; it's Miriam, too. He is tired. He has grown accustomed to only small fits of sleep. He wakes before dawn to be sure she's sleeping and her wounds aren't rubbing against the sheets.

Aaron looks at Miriam's face in the morning light. It was only two months ago that she went off so lighthearted and cheerful to meet Rachel for coffee at Café Atara on Ben Yehuda Street. The sisters ate chocolate cake, drank coffee at a small table under a white umbrella. They had finished their afternoon conversation and were walking to their cars, parked near Zion Square, when the bomb exploded at the Sbarro restaurant. Miriam saw a baby stroller ricochet across the street and break through the window at Frischman's shoe store. The pressure from the explosion forced the sisters to the ground. Miriam had glass cuts along the side of her face. Pieces of something wet and thick were in her hair. After the blast, she reached for Rachel's cell phone and called Aaron. "We're alive. Meet us at Hadassah."

At the hospital, there was screaming. Bells ringing. To be sure the blood on Miriam's shirt wasn't from an open wound on her chest, they cut her blouse, leaving her exposed. Pieces of the sleeves were still wrapped around her wrists. She was wearing a light blue hospital gown. Aaron couldn't find her shoes. Miriam didn't remember who took them. Rachel was down the hall with only minor cuts to her face. Her hip was swollen from the fall.

Late that evening, when they sat in bed together, Miriam said without pretense, "CNN was there. I saw the cameramen. They were waiting, anticipating 'something' would happen." Her eyes were like miniature movie screens, wide enough to show the images of the catastrophe she witnessed. Raw footage was replaying over and over across her sullen face. "We have

CNN to show everything to the world, right?" Her voice wasn't sarcastic or full of anger. It seemed she was almost hopeful CNN would make sense of this insanity, and then everyone outside would understand. Help her understand.

"Yes, Miriam, everyone is watching us." Watching and waiting like parents ready to say "I told you so," he thought. His hands were so cold. He rubbed them together to make heat.

"They stand at our street corners with their cameras loaded, like guns, like our soldiers. With microphones in their hands, dangling wires and weighted down with backpacks, anticipating a death, a slew of deaths, blood, and the wails of the almost dead," Miriam said softly. She adjusted the pillows behind her bandaged shoulder. "They think they're blameless observers, but they are part of this mess, too, you know."

Miriam fell asleep that first night the way she would for months to come, with a sleeping pill. Aaron watched her breath become shallow. He traced the crimson thread-like wound along her hairline, then he closed his eyes until dawn. In those brief moments between sleep and wakefulness, he often saw a flurry of photographs falling. Black-and-white images. Faces that caught his attention.

Yaacov never arrives before 10 A.M., and lately his coffee break in Amina Behari's kitchen across the street has stretched till almost 10:15. It's easier for Aaron to wait in the garden than to call his clients. His summer wedding schedule is full this year. Today he isn't in the mood for pestering mothers of the bride or the already-disappointed mothers-in-law. He prefers waiting in the garden among the bougainvilleas Aliza planted when she and Michael moved here. While he waits, he will clean his camera lenses and rearrange his equipment bag.

Miriam throws back her last sip of tea, leaves her breakfast half eaten and begins weeding and clipping the rose bushes. She learned how to prune and deadhead flowers from Aliza.

Aaron listens to the clip of her shears and hears camera shutters snapping in his head. He grabs his camera. The light is not overhead, and there's little reflection off the smooth stones of the garden wall. He captures images of Miriam leaning into the flowers. He's consumed with the sweep of her back against the wall, the placement of her hands on her hips, the tomatoes uneaten on her plate.

Miriam has grown accustomed to Aaron's spontaneous photo sessions. She knows it will end when the roll of film is completed. Then he takes Miriam's half-eaten cheese and tomatoes and begins his second meal. He eats her food as if she left it intentionally for his consumption.

"Do you ever think about Aliza and Michael returning to Jerusalem? I think she would be proud of my gardening, don't you?" Miriam shelters her eyes from the sun. She's made a quick recovery. There are only a few remaining marks on her face. She was offered a leave of absence from her job at Bank Leumi to rest. She feels much better, she says.

She squints and tilts her head like a child asking permission. "She must want to see Shira's grave. You'd think. I would. I mean, if I were her. Could you stay away from home for so long?" Aaron holds his response just a little too long. It isn't intentional. He doesn't know what to say. Often he doesn't know what to say. He can wait for someone else to speak without worry.

"Don't even bother responding. I'm just running at the mouth today. I'm distracted, too." She fumbles with the radio to hear the news.

The bomb at Sbarro wasn't a beginning; it was just the end of another quiet period. The intifada had begun again. Yesterday, less than three miles from their garden, there were pieces of dead bodies in Zion Square in Ziploc bags. Again, Orthodox Jewish men with long beards, black pants, special vests and eyeglasses searched the surfaces of stones, broken chairs, and along the edges of broken glass. They used tweezers to collect a piece of flesh, a lost finger, a lonely ear. They whispered ancient prayers.

Yet today, Miriam and Aaron are in their garden surrounded by flowers. They are so close to the carnage and the seepage of blood back into the earth. Yesterday there were sirens and horns blaring. Miriam has the radio on, muted, just in case. Just in case they need to do something, like find the gas masks, put the cat in the tent designed for small children. It's been eleven years anticipating another Scud attack, another threat of chemical war. Yet life goes on. Crimson roses. Heliotrope. *Hatzav* white as freshly washed linens.

"It's got to be too painful to come back." Miriam reaches for her cup on the table and sips her tea. She snips more mint from the pot by her foot and drops it into her cup. "No one's going to the Old City now. It isn't safe, and you know it." Aaron stands and walks to the gate, in anticipation that Yaacov might be approaching.

He is silent.

"Aliza wouldn't want you to get hurt, you know. That was never her intention. It's her daughter that's dead. The shillings won't bring her back. It's just her ritual." The words "daughter" and "dead," fractured and pained, slip too easily from Miriam's lips.

"It's my ritual too, Miriam," Aaron says, without looking back to his wife. He surprises himself by his ease in acknowledging that the ritual isn't only for Aliza. He returns to the garden table and can see the harsh taste of words souring in Miriam's throat.

"There's never a good time here," he says. "Never a good time to make assumptions about anything. And only time to see what the day brings. You know that better than I do. When the parcel comes, it will be fine. Don't worry."

All the neighbors at 18 Rav Berlin Street knew when Aliza and Michael Adino moved away, it would trouble the delicate balance of their community. After Shira died, some of the neighbors tried to comfort the Adino's with fresh-cooked food—others took care of the garden, carried their garbage to the Dumpster, and offered to clean their home. But nothing was

44

normal. It was awkward for weeks. The neighbors made attempts at small talk with each other, but it was useless. Everyone was fragile, as if waiting for something to happen. Humor felt disrespectful, and the silence was unnerving. The Adinos closed their world, locking everyone out of their lives. It was as if they sealed apartment 3A from all visitors. They crept deeper into themselves, into grief, away from neighbors and friends and family, away from the light, away from the possibilities of renewing their lives.

Was it a day, a week, a month? Aaron didn't remember. He couldn't stop thinking about them alone in the dark apartment. They kept the blinds closed, with only a single light reflecting through the bathroom window after sunset. No sounds of music, no television. He imagined it so dark, things falling apart, and piles of dirty clothes, dirty dishes, and an unmade bed.

No smells of fresh food cooking. But after some time had passed, late one night, very late, after everyone was asleep and the windows were filled with darkness, Aaron saw them walk away from the building. He had just finished reviewing the final prints from the Habari wedding and was pouring a glass of schnapps. Just a little something to help him get to sleep.

An impulse made him quickly dress and follow them. Aaron was unfamiliar with the sensations forcing him to rush towards Aliza and Michael. Miriam was asleep. It was an invasion of privacy. He knew it, but he was curious, and he was sure he could be quiet. He wouldn't disturb them. He didn't want to talk to them. He just wanted to have an image of their faces. He wanted an expression, a gesture, something. Aaron wanted to see what living after death looked like. That's all. He just wanted a glimpse.

He quickly laced his shoes and without hesitation, grabbed his camera.

They wouldn't know he was watching, he thought. The confusion in his racing mind fed his impulsive desire to see them. He wanted to have an image of their faces. They had become shadows to him, void of features, without contour, without depth. He wanted an expression, eyes, a gesture, to make sense of all this darkness and silence. His heart raced.

Aliza was walking in front, beneath the light across the street. It appeared she had not run a brush through her hair in weeks. Long locks of matted curls framed her face. Her arms remained tightly locked around her waist. Michael was so gaunt and insignificant. He had become just a cool silhouette.

He followed their ghosts to Shira's primary school. At first, he couldn't imagine where they were going. But the school was only a few blocks away. In the dark, they sat in the children's swings and rocked back and forth without sharing a word, without a sound. That's all they did. They didn't speak. They didn't touch each other. After a time they just went home. So overwhelmed by their silence, the darkness they shared, Aaron forgot he had brought his camera with him. He stood in the shadows of a tall cypress tree, watched them depart, and waited. It was too early for the morning delivery trucks and too late for anyone to walk the streets after a movie or a drink at the bar. There was only the sound of the cypress leaves rustling in the dry breeze.

A few days passed, and Aaron was startled to see Aliza standing on her sun porch as he was taking his camera equipment to the car. He put his bags against the wall to see if she looked different in the light of day. Instinctively, he closed his left eye and with his right hand formed a scope to create a tight frame around her. It was a rare moment. She hadn't been outside during the day. He called up to her, "Can I visit with you? Bring you mint tea?"

She nodded. "No. No. I'll meet you in the garden. I want to see if our roses are in bloom." Aaron quickly returned to the kitchen and prepared a tray of tea and biscuits. The water boiled quickly. When he returned to the garden, Aliza was pulling dead leaves off of the rosebushes and stuffing them into her pant pockets. He offered tea. They sat together for a few moments before Aliza asked, "Why did you follow us the other night?"

Aaron's dark complexion couldn't hide the color rushing to his face. His bushy eyebrows crested like half moons over his downcast eyes. There was only the sound of a bus shifting gear as it approached their street. "I don't know," Aaron said. He was embarrassed. He couldn't look at her. He grabbed his camera from the bag leaning against the wall and began loading it with film to keep his hands busy. He looked towards the gate, hoping no one would enter. The sun was in his eyes now. He squinted to see her profile.

"Michael and I are leaving," Aliza mumbled, her eyes fixed on the cat sunning on his back at the entrance to the garden. "It isn't just about Shira dying . . . It's about the memories."

Aaron began stuttering, "Yea, yea . . . yes . . . Must be so hard to leave." His breath seemed to fall between syllables and snag the flow of his words.

Aliza's face grew flushed and her hands curled into tight fists. She closed her eyes and with a sharp low voice, she said, "They say dreams don't smell . . . but mine do. I smell death and life fighting in a dimly lit school auditorium crowded with families waiting for a performance." Her voice was sharp and nervous. "The rows are filled and only a few seats remain empty for those standing alone in the aisles. I can't sit with my daughter, and I am scared I will lose her again and again."

Aliza opened her eyes, wet with tears, and slowly scanned each plant in the garden. The rosebushes were in full bloom, their crimson petals reaching upward. The purple irises were lean and tall, with a dark black and silver area below each beard. "It seems you always have your camera with you, Aaron. I have always liked that about you. It must feel like a part of your body."

Aaron adjusted the lens cover and placed the camera on the table. He felt exposed, as if Aliza drew attention to his weakness. It was confusing. He didn't understand why he wasn't proud.

Aliza left the table and walked around the garden. She floated her hands across all the flowerpots as if to record the sensation of each plant's petals and leaves. She brought the bougainvillea close to her face and inhaled their sweet scent. "Before we leave, will you photograph me in this garden? I am a little embarrassed to ask. Not a wedding picture. Something informal, you know, simple."

Aaron was speechless. Aliza slowly walked over to the garden gate. He picked up his camera and adjusted the lens to focus on her. He caught her sweeping her hand across her face to shove back her red curls. She was acting so clear and resolved. Aaron saw a small bird returning to its nest in the background of the photo he was about to shoot. He took ten quick shots in succession. It suddenly dawned on him that this leaving meant Aliza and Michael couldn't visit Shira's grave each *yartzeit.* The sound of the camera shutter snapped again for a few moments and then he was finished with the roll of film. He went to retrieve another roll from his office.

"Aaron, wait one moment." She placed her hand on his shoulder and stood close to his side. Aaron turned to her and saw in her emerald eyes a darkness that could have been misunderstood as grief. But it was a clarity and resolve saved for those who have once been bathed in death. "I have been thinking. I won't be coming to Shira on her *yartzeit.*"

He stood and placed her hand in between his palms and brought it close to his heart. "If you send a shilling each year, I will take it to her grave."

Yaacov knows Aaron will hear his voice in the garden. He doesn't need to ring the buzzer. He rearranges the stacks of fluttering mail between his cragged fingers and the bundles tucked under his sweating armpits and his soft rippling chin. He knows Aaron will meet him in the vestibule soon after he enters.

Aaron is thinking about the shilling, the size of tea biscuit, wrapped in a thin piece of plastic bubble wrap, sealed with layers of shiny electrical tape. Each shilling is carved with images of dancing flowers and Aliza's fingerprints—subtle rings of fine lines hinting at her delicate touch.

As he promised Aliza decades ago, on Shira's *yartzeit*, always before dawn, before the buses fill the streets of Jerusalem, Aaron walks to the Mount of Olives from his apartment in Rehavia. He takes Aza Street, winding past the President's House, past the embassies, down to the Kings Hotel to the Jaffa Road intersection.

From this point, it's not a long walk down into the valley, through Mamila to the Jaffa Gate. Several times he has thought to go through the gates, to enter the enclosed walls and to trek through the alleys of the Arab quarter to reach the Lion's Gate from the inside of the ancient fortress. However, he doesn't deviate from his journey; he paces himself through the narrow walkways, confronting the city's mysterious grip. He is sure the shillings were meant for such a journey through the Jewish quarter. They were meant to wander through the veins and entrails of religion's earthy body.

Aaron walks past the grounds of King David's City above the Arab villages nested in the valley. He doesn't drive to the Mount of Olives because he believes this journey on foot is sacred. Aliza offered him this blessed rite, and he does it without question or doubt.

He likes to hold the shilling in the palm of his hand and listen to the sands and rocks crush beneath his feet. He likes to feel the pulse of his breath mix with the smells of the morning and the images of golden light reflecting off the stones of the city. He walks through the same ascending rows of graves to reach Shira's marker. *Shira Adino, daughter of Michael ben Joseph and Aliza bat Abraham. Born in Jerusalem April 19, 1960, died in Maa'lot May 5, 1973. May God comfort you among the mourners of Zion and Jerusalem.*

The shillings remain scattered from year to year on her grave marker. No one touches them. No one takes them away. They replace the traditional memorial stone. On sunny days, they glisten in the early morning light, reflecting circles of colored rings around the grave. When it rains, the shillings sparkle.

After Aaron says Kaddish, the mourner's prayer, in a

singular motion, uninterrupted by reflex or second thoughts, he slides the *kippah* from his head down the side of his face, across his heart, into his right pocket. He opens his left palm to the sunlight. Aliza's love stone glimmers and shines. He places it on Shira's grave and leaves her alone with her mother's whispers and passion. Aaron feels a sacred embrace between the women. He turns away. Not to intrude. Not to indulge. He is just the messenger.

Aaron wears a miserable expression throughout the day. It is the end of the month and the shilling still hasn't arrived. Yaacov nods to Aaron and lifts his shoulders with a sad resolve. He has nothing to offer Aaron. There's no parcel from Aliza. The day before the *yartzeit*, Aaron and Miriam agree they had better call her.

Aaron sits by the phone for a few moments before he makes the call. It has been many years since they have spoken. Aliza writes, but he hasn't talked to Michael in a long time. He doesn't know what he will say, but the urgency to call consumes him.

"Michael? It's Aaron here . . . in Jerusalem. It's been some time. How are you and Aliza? All is well?"

"You haven't heard," Michael says.

Aaron doesn't speak.

Michael continues, "Aliza died last month." Michael stops for a moment and seems to compose himself. "It really was so unexpected. Everything seemed to be going as usual, and then she just didn't wake up one morning."

Aaron signals Miriam to come to the phone. His hand is flapping in the air, like a sparrow caught in the brush. He wants her to press her ear to the receiver with him and listen to Michael. He doesn't want to have to say out loud, "Aliza is dead."

Miriam offers their condolences, expresses their shock. Her voice breaks and folds before Aaron can ask about the shilling. Michael says he didn't know about the shillings until a few days ago when he was sorting through her belongings and found a package ready to be mailed.

"I am sorry . . . I meant to call sooner. It's just there were so many things to do. I should have called you." Michael paused again for an uncomfortable silence. "I found in the package a shilling and a letter addressed to you. Aliza wrote she had changed her mind. She was ready to come back to Jerusalem. She said she was ready to go home," Michael says.

After exchanging a few words with Michael, questions about Aliza's funeral in America, inquiries about his family, and a few more niceties, they say they'll talk soon. Miriam follows Aaron out into the garden. "He didn't say he was coming home, did he? He didn't bury her here, with Shira," she mutters.

Aaron is pacing, his hands deep in his pant pockets, rattling his keys against loose change. His downcast eyes search wildly for patterns within the floor tiles. He jerks his hands to the top of his head and pulls his hair to the nape of his neck. Back and forth, jerking his scalp.

"Aaron, are you okay? What can I do for you?"

He walks back into the apartment and heads down the hall to his office. Speechless. He starts riffling through the piles of papers on his desk. He looks for the parcel. Piles of contact sheets fall to the floor. Books neatly stacked against the wall tumble off of the desk. There are pictures of brides, mothers, women's faces scattered on the floor.

"Aaron, what are you doing?"

No answer. He doesn't want to look to her or hear her voice.

She waits. She tries to understand what he's looking for, what he's doing.

"Aaron, I'm talking to you." Her arms wrap tightly around her waist. "What are you doing?" She approaches him. She leans toward him, placing her hands on his shoulders to contain him, to offer him comfort. He shrugs his shoulders and pushes her away.

"I'm really confused. I know that shilling came this year. Wasn't it gold this year? I know I saw the parcel, and I misplaced it. I must have misplaced it, Miriam."

"Aaron, what are you doing? What are you looking for?" Miriam is confused.

"It must be here. I saw it here on my desk. The shilling was on my desk, and I misplaced it. I'll find it. This year the shilling is gold. I remember it is gold this year. I'll find it now." Aaron is agitated. Sweat drips from his forehead. His shirt is sticking to his wet skin.

"Aaron, it's over. You've got to stop this. The shilling isn't here. Please. Please come and sit down with me."

He digs into his file cabinet, then opens and shuts each desk drawer, once, twice, three times before he starts pulling out the books from the shelves along the wall. Aaron turns around and, in a fluid motion, slams his hand on the desk and screams, "Shut up, Miriam. Just shut up and get the hell out of here. I am going to find it!"

Miriam sleeps for several hours into the early afternoon. She walks into the garden and sees in the distance Yaacov delivering mail up the hill. He has been to their building already. Aaron is sitting at the table in the garden; today's mail strewn across the white surface. It's afternoon and the sun is overhead, filling the sky with a dusty heat, leaving the Judean hills hiding in a yellow fog. Aaron gets up and prepares an iced tea with mint for her. Their silence is full of denial. It is the moment when grieving hasn't yet set in, and the mind still believes there's another story to be told. Aaron feels his body searching for a sensation to prove his heart wrong.

"Maybe you should come with me to Shira's grave?" Aaron murmurs. He looks at her and she can see his eyes are swollen, his face sore and twisted. "We could take the pictures of Aliza. The pictures I took of her out here, under the olive tree. I took them over there, do you remember?"

As Aaron speaks, a wave of relief washes over Miriam. Her shoulders release. Her hands, clenched against her mouth, start to flatten. "Yes, of course, Aaron. I don't want to wait till

tomorrow, do you?" Miriam knows it sounds impulsive, absurd
to go now, to just get up and go walking to the Old City when
it is so hot. "If it gets too late, it'll be difficult to find Shira. We
should go now."

Under the heat of the late day's sun, Aaron and Miriam
walk to the Mount of Olives. They appear as if they are headed
for a late-afternoon picnic. Aaron carries a full pack and two
bottles of water. Miriam's arms are full of flowers from the
garden, and she is wearing a backpack, too. Climbing through
rows of grave markers, it's easy to find Shira's grave. She lies
beneath a cover of glistening shillings, shining bright, a crest
of color in a sea of dry white stones. Miriam places a bouquet
of flowers on her grave. They sit beside Shira for a while before
they can hold hands, before they can talk.

Aaron brings pictures of Aliza and an envelope of letters
and news articles he saved about the Maa'lot massacre. There
is no breeze. Aaron takes the papers out and places them on
her grave. They do not move. They do not flutter.

The cover page from *Ha'aretz* and *The International Herald
Tribune.* May 1973. Bold black lettering. Harsh headlines describing
the massacre. Articles retelling the details of the slaughter.
Pictures of parents falling into arms of family as they bury their
dead children. Hands clutched around screaming mouths. Heads
arched backwards. Closed eyes. Faces soaked in tears.

Miriam wrote a letter to the editor of the *Ha'aretz* newspaper
after the massacre. Aaron saved it. "Miriam, do you want to
read this?" He hands her the faded news clipping.

Miriam looks at the letter, then at Aaron. It has been so
long since she has seen it. She can no longer hold back her tears.
"Aaron, please read it for me. I can't, I just can't do it now."

> *To the Editor:*
> *I am a friend of Aliza and Michael Adino. They are the
> parents of Shira Adino, murdered at the Field School in Maa'lot.
> I am not writing this letter for them, but about them and about*

all of us who don't understand what is happening to our country.

I don't know anymore if it matters that Prime Minister Meir promised to protect our children. She couldn't and she didn't. In the end, when she negotiated and offered to give them back all twenty-three prisoners of war in exchange for our children, it didn't make a difference.

It wasn't enough for them. It's never enough here for anyone. Will it make a difference in the end that the negotiations fell apart when children, terrorists, couldn't remember their directions? What 'code word,' what message, would have been easy to remember? They say some code word from their leaders would have called off the mission. It could have been aborted, they say. They were too young, too scared, they didn't get the message, they say. Will anyone remember there was a message at Maa'lot?

Miriam HaLev, Rehavia, Jerusalem

Miriam curls into Aaron's arms and cries. Aaron is afraid. It's not the kind of fear that overcame him when he found her alive in the emergency room this spring. This fear swells in his belly and burns. This time he isn't scared for Miriam's life, this time he's frightened he has reached an end. An end with no new beginning in sight. What next? What now?

Aaron reaches into the envelope containing the photographs and retrieves small handwritten pages. He adds them to the mosaic blanket of newspaper clippings and letters, photographs. Pictures of Shira as a child. Aliza gardening. Michael and Aliza holding their baby when she was a newborn.

Children are coming home from school now. The sound of small voices singing and laughing in the streets below surround them, wrap them into a tight hold. The sun is beginning to descend, yet it is still so hot and bright. As Miriam opens her umbrella for shade, the arid breeze flips the letters and news clippings, forcing them to fly off the grave. They fall down the hillside, floating off into the distance. Neither Miriam nor Aaron moves to chase the falling paper. Only the photos remain unmoved. The prints shine in the sunlight. Aaron begins to collect the images and puts them back into the envelope. He places the closed envelope at the base of the grave marker and puts the pile of shillings on top of it. Glistening shillings. Cobalt. Crimson. Jade and gold. They eat and drink their water. Miriam dozes with her head in Aaron's lap.

Hours have passed. From above the Old City, Aaron and Miriam witness the pious congregating at the Western Wall for evening prayers. Streams of dark-clothed men and women, children in a flurry around them, crowd and press their faces against the smooth stone surface. From the Al Aqsa Mosque, just above the crowds, the mullah is offering his call to evening prayers. Lines of men and small boys are walking up the hill to their holy shrine.

Dusk. Pink skies and evening breezes. The walls of the city are golden. With the setting sun and the approaching darkness, the stones brighten and come alive with a butter yellow luster.

From the top of the Mount of Olives, in the company of rows and rows of flat grave markers, Aaron and Miriam are embraced by souls floating in streaming waxed light. Aaron sees his photographs of Aliza, one after another, then every wedding, every bar mitzvah, every family portrait he ever created with parents, aunts, uncles, and cousins, with fleeting smiles and hopeful eyes, slipping away without a sound. He sees swirling faded sepia-tone images searching for the parched land, rippled with gentle hills and lonesome rocks. The faces in each photograph disappear as they approach the endless dusty horizon.

There is the faint scent of eucalyptus. Aaron reaches for Miriam's hand and for that moment he is no longer waiting. The summer heat is retreating into the evening breeze that sweeps through the seven hills of Jerusalem and off to the Judean desert. For now, it is all there is.

BIRDHOUSES

Ben Gebhardt

I can remember being suspended from my seatbelt, looking down at her. She was unconscious, but her lower jaw hung open as though paused before telling me something important. Soon blood began to trickle down her forehead from a split just below her hairline, and I realized we were in an emergency. But before that, when it was just me looking at my mother about to speak, I felt peaceful, ready to listen. She was wearing jeans, still a deep indigo, and a puffy powder blue coat with chrome snaps. Her hair was a respectable balance of gray and dark brown, with a single lock fallen forward beside her sharp nose, altogether, at that moment, I thought she looked very rational, maybe even a little bit wise, and then the blood came.

My mother's divorce—that was how I thought of it,

something she owned, like a kettle or a purse—occupied no space in my mind and had nothing to do with why I had visited her. I went because I worried she was getting loony out on the peninsula, becoming some kind of eccentric. The sort of person you see from your car and feel sure you'll never know, because all of your friends are so normal, so level. I planned to go as a stabilizing force, a touchstone to the rational world if indeed she was that far gone.

The day of the accident, I was angry with her. I was angry with what she was letting herself become, and I didn't have the guts to say anything about it. I just smiled as she explained her birdhouses to me. We had finally gotten into the car when she began her discourse. She had chosen this craft as the object of her unraveling, she made and made and made these cubic houses from pine boards and painted them in solid colors with the glossiest paints available—orange, purple, lemon, lime, fuchsia. They looked like fruit chews hanging on the trees in her backyard. If she had been a man, perhaps it would have been young women instead of birdhouses—bright, glossy girls, one after the other, and I might have been okay with that, because I craved something normal, some kind of depravity that was labeled and well known.

But the birdhouses disgusted me. I can remember the feeling as she talked to me in the car, feeling sick beneath the anger, like I was somehow implicated by her neurosis.

She made boxes for birds. They weren't houses except by some great abstraction of the term. She had spent the morning cutting a 1' x 8' into squares. Enough wood for two bird boxes. After two hours of the sports channel, I joined her in the garage, watched her trim lengths of dowels for the perches. Her methodic cuts annoyed me. She had a little jig set up to establish the appropriate length, then three slow passes with the Japanese handsaw and another perch dropped onto the workbench. She arranged these as she progressed in two neat rows. I watched for ten minutes not knowing whether or not she knew I was there.

I tried to keep the contempt out of my voice. "Hey Mom, why don't you take a break for a bit?"

She wasn't the least bit startled when I spoke. She kept her head down and said, "Let me finish with these dowels, honey, then we can drive to town for lunch."

I nodded and hit the garage-door opener. The gray brightness of a hazy morning drowned out the incandescent light above her workbench. I walked out to the driveway and looked across the road. I had forgotten how thick the forest was around her. Just down from her house two giant cedars seemed to reign over the firs that packed in around them. They grew so close together that their foliage was indistinguishable. Red, stringy bark encrusted the trunks like barnacles on sea rocks. They seemed as ancient as rocks to me, bark and soft flat needles perpetually sloughing off while their core remained.

Her hands were a tiny bit shaky. She was no master of the craft, and I could tell the sharp little saw made her nervous. Perspiration was building up on her forehead and in front of her ears. In the corner of the garage a dozen of the boxes were stacked, waiting for paint. I tried not to think about how much time she must have spent out here.

I drove us in her car that day, an old blue and silver Japanese hatchback with brittle vinyl seats and dull paint. It had started to rain lightly, and the road had gone from gray to a deep charcoal color. I brought the aging car up to speed on the two-lane highway and had to hug the right side of my lane to diminish the blast of air as a truck sped by. There is a sawmill fifteen miles past my mother's house that receives a dozen or so logging trucks a day. They all seem to accelerate wildly through this last semi-unpopulated stage of the drive. My mother talked to me as I drove the winding road toward town. The Doug firs were dense on either side of the road and reached high above the earth—I couldn't see the tops through the cramped windshield.

She started in about the birdhouses again, this time

positioning her hands above the dashboard displaying one plane and then the next of her craft pieces. She talked about symmetry and the pros and cons of using knotty pine. It paints well, and she can select pieces with large knots to knock out for the doorway, she said, but it can warp on her unexpectedly, destroying the tidy look she's after. What was it I felt in my throat as she spoke? Something sickening, confirming, an oily taste that felt like hunger and nausea simultaneously.

It wasn't the fact of her woodworking as much as the way she talked about it. Like I should understand, or rather, *understood* what she was going for with her craft. My reaction was almost entirely physical, somewhat dizzy, removing me from the actual steering of the car. We were taking a long curve to the right that seemed endless in the thick forest, and the car was edging closer to the centerline. I was vaguely aware of this, but from a distance, from somewhere outside of the vehicle.

The oncoming truck blasted an air horn just as our wheels crossed into the paint. Suddenly back, I jerked the wheel to the right and somehow missed the truck. The car was sideways for a split second as all four tires lost traction. In a moment they would grip the asphalt and flip the little hatchback into the air for one silent, spinning second before we landed passenger side down, skidding to the side of the road like an upturned brick. Before we went airborne, I remember looking at my mother and feeling guilty, as though it was something deliberate I had done. But she was far away from me. Her eyes were shut and she looked more sad than afraid. Her hands were flat on the dashboard and her posture was apologetic, and then the car lurched violently off the ground.

I had no way of broaching the distance, of knowing what was behind her eyelids. I could feel my hands against the steering wheel, tight and violent, shameful.

In the emergency room, all I could do was focus on what the doctor was telling me. It had taken an hour for my mother to regain consciousness, and both her arms were apparently paralyzed.

The doctor took me out to the corridor to talk; he was overly congenial, almost fatherly. "I have to say it's a bit mysterious. The x-rays came back completely normal and show no sign of spinal or shoulder injury. Apart from the obvious, there's really nothing to indicate any damage was done to the nervous tissue."

I looked at the door to my mother's hospital room, before responding to the doctor. "Yeah, but the 'obvious' is that she can't move her arms, and she doesn't feel it when we touch her. So what is that—is this all psycho stuff or what?" I could feel a twisting in my stomach as I thought of my mother's wood shop. The doctor had not wanted to talk in front of her. She was that delicate.

"Your mother has what appears to be a psychosomatic paralysis. But I have to believe it is temporary—shock related. The psychological trauma of the accident was overwhelming and her mind is choosing this—temporarily—to cope."

I stared at him. I wanted to know how long it would take. I wanted to go back to work. I didn't want to be stuck on the peninsula taking care of her like this. My ears were hot and my stomach chilled as I thought about staying.

"Her arms will come back, Tom, her reflexes are all there . . ."

I worked at a mechanical engineering firm in Seattle. I rented a one-bedroom apartment in an overpriced brick building a stone's throw from a plethora of clubs, bars, and cafés, whose noise soothed me to sleep at night. Financially speaking, I should have been looking at getting into a house, but I loved the hubbub. As a rule I never went out in my neighborhood. I drank beer at upscale bars downtown before I came home, if I felt the need. I'd sit with my fellow men, my peers—though I was the most junior among them—and talk about sprinkler systems and college football, sewage problems, the horror stories of design flaw. At home, the noise from the populous streets nearby provided an antidote for loneliness without having to be with anyone; it filled the space around me until I was safely asleep.

I played basketball on Tuesdays and Thursdays. I ran the steep flanks of Queen Anne hill once a week—three times on an especially good week. There were times when I hiked with old friends from college. I had a life to get back to.

My mother didn't know anyone on the peninsula very well. She had moved out there five years ago and kept to herself at work, never saw the need for friends, I guess. She had consigned herself to a state of meditative loneliness, and now I was going to have to pay for it. We were released after six hours at the ER. The doctor gave me the number of a physical therapist to call if her arms weren't back in a couple of days.

We sat on a concrete bench waiting for a cab to show up. The doctor had put her coat back on for her, and we sat side by side without talking. Pigeons crowded a nearby trash can in the twilight. Her arms hung into her lap, palms up on the thighs of her jeans. I watched her hands, anticipating movement.

"You trying to move them?"

She shook her head slowly, without speaking. I thought of talking to her about her birdhousing. My dad had a complete wood shop in the garage when I was growing up. He wanted to teach me everything he knew along this line, and I remember many Saturdays spent listening to him drone on about safety with the power tools. We always wore plastic eye goggles and dust masks. We pushed boards through the table saw together, slicing long thin strips off the sides. It's called a rip when you cut a board parallel with the grain. My mother and father ripped apart this way.

My mother would flick the lights off and on when she wanted us to come in for lunch, rather than try to make herself heard over the saw. I always thought it annoyed her; all the cutting, the dust, and the long hours of concentrated silence. It all seemed intolerable to her. It was for me. When I made it to high school, I realized I could decline my father's invitations, and I never joined in again. He was a fabulous woodworker. He made a rocking chair one summer and even carved the backboard with a kind of sunburst that was perpetually rising or setting in a choppy sea. But there was a tyranny in his work, too. His rules, his decisions, he didn't take suggestions. I envied my mother for never having to be subjected to the repetitive teachings on tool maintenance and respect for your materials. She was smart about it, she would flick the lights and by the time I looked up, she was gone.

I fixed a can of instant soup and spooned it into her mouth for dinner. The silence between us was thick. It seemed to emanate from her lifeless arms and fill the house. The paralysis wasn't real. The doctor had said that. *Move your arms, Mom.*

I wasn't in the habit of drinking tea, but I was struck with a memory of my mother drinking tea and reading late at night, so I offered. I fumbled in her kitchen, finding the right accouterments, feeling sudden washes of familiarity when I came across old utensils, so that opening drawers in there was like looking through a photo album. The teapot was one of their wedding gifts. It had a copper bottom and a black plastic lid, spring-loaded over the spout. It was the kind where the spout is the only opening. As I filled it with water, I realized that in all my life, I'd never done that. Never held back the lid, never had to peer in, listen for the rising pitch as the water filled in the dark space.

I tipped the cup to her lips. She blinked when she'd had enough. We didn't speak to each other, we focused on the physical task. I helped her change into her pajamas, undressing and dressing. These things I hadn't thought of. The bra. The toilet. I wiped her, pulled up her pants. I told myself she had done this for me. I told myself I did this to her.

It was Saturday night and the quiet of the guest room drilled into me as I lay awake. Both of them, my mother and father, now loomed before me practicing their carpentry. They seemed static and diminished in my mind, like an empty set of bookends. And this was my place now, between them. The sudden awareness of my frailty was frightening: the trembling water of her teapot, rising in pitch.

It was Monday before my mother got out of bed. I called my work and the elementary school where she was a nurse and told them what had happened: I was stuck, she was stuck, until further notice. I wasn't planning on waiting long.

I called the physical therapist immediately after we ate breakfast. The earliest I could get an appointment was the end of the week, but they said to move her arms as much as possible in the meantime, for circulation. I looked at her when I hung up the phone. She was slumped on the sofa, still in her green pajamas—darkened at the chest from where I spilled a spoonful of cereal on her and had to clean it with a wet sponge. Her arms looked boneless at her sides.

"The PT said we should move your arms around so your lymphatic vessels will keep going and the tendons and all that. Here." I crouched in front of her and lifted her arms up and down like she was dribbling basketballs. "Can you feel that?"

She shook her head and sighed, watching her arms swimming in front of her. Her lips curved into a smile and she said, "This is ridiculous, Tom."

I ignored her. I wanted the whole thing to be over. I kept going, watching her shoulder joints and then her eyes, half-expecting her arms to kick-start from the movement. After a minute I stopped and said, "Unless you have a better idea, I think we'll just have to do that once in a while."

She nodded and turned toward the window. There were maybe two dozen birds scattered on the yard and among the fir trees, scouting out what remained of the seed. Where the

Steller's jays perched on some of the orange enameled cubes, their bright blue feathers crackled with contrast. She watched the birds come and go between the forest and the many colored boxes for the rest of the day.

I watched TV and shook her arms out once an hour. There was nothing else I could do. After dinner I couldn't take it anymore. She seemed too complacent, like she wasn't even trying, just watching the birds. I bent at the waist and grabbed her wrists, dragging one at a time into the air. She glanced at me and then looked back to the darkening forest.

I threw her arms down and said, "Come on, Mom! There is nothing wrong with your arms. Everything's connected, okay? You have to do this with me."

"Nothing's wrong except I can't move them, you mean." She looked around the house, appealing for support. "I don't care what the tests say, I can't make my hands move. I tell them to over and over, and they lay there like they don't know me." She leaned forward as she talked and then heaved back against the couch between her motionless arms.

It was all I could do not to yell at her. "Look, Ma," I growled, "I need to go back to work and so do you, okay? Stop watching the damn birds and try to move your arms. You are not paralyzed. It's in your head." I pointed at my head for emphasis and glared. My father made this gesture, usually indicating something was inexplicably crooked in the person he was talking to. She recognized it before I did.

She turned back to the windows, now nothing more than dark mirrors reflecting her living room. She said, "Tom, those birds are free in a way that you and I can never understand freedom. I try to approach that. I'm trying to learn something, okay?" She was looking at me in the black reflection of the window, "If you want to be like your Dad, that's fine, but you'll never get to be you, and someday you'll want to."

My stomach twisted, bilious and tight. "What are you talking about, Ma? I'm not the one with a wood shop in my garage making stupid bird boxes!" My heart thumped audibly as I spoke to her; I could feel the blood flaming up my neck. All the disgust swelled up in my head and I wanted to kick something.

My mother's face trembled, the rest of her was motionless. "Thomas, you will not speak to me like that in my house," there were tears on her face now. "You don't even know what you're talking about—how could you? You never even bother to think about it!" She shook her head to get the tears from her eyes, sending ripples down her dead arms. "It's true. I miss him. I'll never be the same without him. He's good at things, Tom."

I was silent. Suddenly her divorce had ripped open the ground beneath me, and I fell in. It was a place she'd been before; I could see that. A place she'd climbed out of once, that I never knew was there. It lay beneath me these many years and now swallowed me up. I had to keep an eye on her for balance; the living room was threatening to spin upside down. She continued to talk and cry.

"But he's not good with me, all right? He'll never be good with me. Never." And here she began to bounce her hand on the seat cushion beside her while she sobbed, "Never, never, never," and she was gasping for air, wiping tears from her eyes with her delicately thin, calloused fingers. She looked at the ceiling and swallowed, wiping her fingers on her shirt.

I saw that her arms were working again, but I was too overwhelmed to speak. I backed away from the couch and left her there, breathing heavily, looking up. I found myself outside on the granulated asphalt of her driveway. I shivered with loneliness when I looked at the trees. They spread out beneath the vast clouded sky like a cold, multitudinous army. The wind whirred between the branches of the cedars and the firs. It seemed there were not enough trees in the world to fill the space around me.

SWEET DREAMS

Mary Bruno

"This is just a clear gel that helps conduct the electrical signals from your brain," said Walter, flashing the small white tube of ElectraLube on cue. He glanced across the room at Evelyn, who was giving the electrodes one last alcohol swab. He was intent on projecting the air of a seasoned professional, but his spindly palms were damp, and if he had glanced in the mirror above the bed, he would have seen insecurity in his pale gray eyes.

"It washes right off with soap and water," he continued. "We'll put a little on the electrodes before we tape them in place."

Walter had heard Evelyn give this little talk half a dozen times now. He was amazed at how fresh she could make it sound. Walter wasn't used to working with human subjects. He spent his time with rats. He'd have to work on his delivery.

Mrs. Nancy Turlikowski sat stiffly on the edge of the bed. Her round face was placid, almost mask-like. Her eyes were closed. She smelled like baby powder and toothpaste. Mrs. T was a referral. The lab took individual cases like hers occasionally, usually as a favor for one of Dr. Dante's colleagues. Dr. Dante (his first name was Lorenzo, but as far as Walter knew, nobody ever called him that) was Walter's boss, the lab's principal investigator.

Dr. Dante was an extraordinarily paranoid man. He expected the worst and prepared for it, an approach that made him somewhat unpleasant as a human being but one of the most successful sleep researchers in the country. Dr. Dante was the reason why Walter and, for that matter, Mrs. T, were here in the sleep chamber at ten o'clock on a Friday night.

Walter was supposed to be finishing up his first year in medical school by now. His plan was to be a cardiac surgeon, or maybe a psychiatrist. But he was rejected by every medical school he applied to. Eight schools and not even an interview. Walter accepted Dr. Dante's job offer the day the last school turned him down. The lab hadn't been his first choice, but he was thrilled to be working for such a well-known scientist and relieved to have a well-paying job. He had learned a great deal in his nine months at the sleep lab. Very soon now, Walter would have to reconsider his future. The deadline for submitting medical school applications was six weeks away.

For now, Walter was focused on Mrs. T. She was a 34-year-old assistant manager in the frozen foods section of the local A&P. For more than a year now, Mrs. T had been suffering from horrible nightmares. The nightmares were causing insomnia, which in turn was affecting her work. The store manager had already had a talk with Mrs. T about her lack of focus. Her doctor was stumped. He referred her to a neurologist who had gone to medical school with Dr. Dante. The neurologist ordered two EEGs and a CAT scan. He prescribed medication, hypnosis, and finally psychotherapy. When the nightmares persisted, the neurologist consulted Dr. Dante, who offered to conduct a two-night sleep analysis. Tonight was Mrs. T's first night in the chamber.

As he taped the electrodes tenderly to Mrs. T's forehead and temples and under her chin, Walter told her all about the sleep chamber. It was an electrically insulated four-room suite. Dr. Dante held a patent on its design. From the outside, the chamber looked like an oversized bank vault. On the inside, each room was set up just like this one: a twin bed, a nightstand with a reading lamp, and a large one-way mirror above the bed so that the researchers could peek in on subjects—Mrs. T's eyelids shot open—which, Walter assured her, they almost never did.

"Do people ever have trouble getting to sleep?" she asked, carefully scratching her right temple at a point just below the electrode.

"Never," said Evelyn, from behind Mrs. T.

Evelyn came around the bed and stood beside Walter. Placing a hand on Evelyn's shoulder, Walter told Mrs. T that she could thank Evelyn here for the old movie posters on the walls and for the vase of carnations beside the bed. Personally, Walter had no idea how anybody could get to sleep in the chamber's dreary windowless cells, but he kept that opinion to himself. As he showed Mrs. T the headboard with its built-in circuit panel where he would plug in her electrodes, Evelyn leaned in to inspect his handiwork. When she was satisfied that all electrodes were securely in place, she strode to the door.

"If you need anything, we'll be right outside," Evelyn told Mrs. T. With a hitchhiker's jerk of her thumb, she motioned Walter out of the room. "Sleep well," said Evelyn cheerily, and switched off the light.

As Walter entered the lab he slipped off his white lab coat and tossed it over the top of the wooden coat rack next to the door. He turned to face Evelyn.

"How'd I do?" he asked, stuffing his hands into the pockets of his blue jeans. He shifted his weight back and forth from one foot to the other. Evelyn put her fingers to her lips and leaned back against the thick gray door of the sleep chamber until she heard the soft click. The door shielded the chamber from any stray electrical signals that might be zinging around.

"You're a natural," she said, lying.

Walter grinned.

Walter followed Evelyn to the bank of polygraphs that stood against the wall outside the sleep chamber. There were four, one for each room. Walter loved the six-foot-high steel towers. These humming, blinking behemoths stood guard over the subjects and kept Walter and Evelyn company all night long. Their top panel was a riot of knobs and dials and lights and toggle switches. There was a two-door cabinet at the bottom where Evelyn stored the giant boxes of polygraph paper and the extra sets of electrodes. In between, about waist high, was the flat surface where the white graph paper passed slowly beneath six ink pens. Each pen recorded the impulses from one of the electrodes Walter had just attached to Mrs. T. The pens would map her gradual descent into the valley of sleep. The constant scratch-scratch was the soundtrack of her journey.

Walter told Evelyn about a dream he'd had that afternoon: he was at a party in his old frat house, hiding in a shower stall to escape two predatory coeds.

"You should be so lucky," said Evelyn, adjusting the amplitude on the polygraph.

After twenty years at the lab, Evelyn could tell which stage of sleep a patient was entering by the sound of the pens. Mrs. T's journey would begin with antic etchings, like mice nesting in the walls. This was the sound of the alpha brain waves that signaled her drowsy slide into unconsciousness. Slow sweeps of the pens heralded stages 3 and 4, the delta rhythms of deep repose that Mrs. T wouldn't reach for three or more hours after lights out. Six or so hours in, as she emerged from the deepest cavern of stage 4, she'd start to dream. Her darting eyes would send the pens into the spastic jig of REM, the rapid eye movement phase—dreamland. Her dreaming would begin as fleeting, seconds-long bursts, then stretch gradually into feature-length episodes—forty-five minutes or more—longer than it took Walter to drive to work.

"We'll have to stay alert for REM with this one," Evelyn told Walter. She was squatting in front of the polygraph adjusting the paper feed while Walter topped off the inkwells. He admired the way her brown polyester pants clung to the lumps in her hips.

Walter and Evelyn usually took their lunch break after the last patient was hooked up and tucked in. Since there was only one patient tonight, lunch started early. Walter headed down the hall to the soda machine and returned with two Diet Pepsis for Evelyn and a ginger ale for himself. They spread their food out on the large desk near the polygraphs. Evelyn had her usual: salad and yogurt, raspberry yogurt tonight. Walter was on a liverwurst sandwich kick.

Evelyn propped her feet up on an overturned wastebasket. She was wearing black, heavy-soled oxfords, the kind favored by nurses and waitresses and people recovering from bunion surgery. Evelyn was a nurse.

"Is Mrs. T's problem serious?" asked Walter as he unwrapped his sandwich.

"Nobody really knows," said Evelyn. She shrugged. "The neurologist had her on iridimine for a while. It's a REM suppressant. He figured, you know, if she spent less time dreaming, she'd have fewer nightmares, but it just got worse. Dante thinks she's a head case."

"What do you think?" asked Walter.

Evelyn lifted a forkful of lettuce to her mouth.

"I think the smell of that sandwich is making me sick."

Walter knew that Mrs. T's nightmares, while intriguing, were not the lab's main focus. Dr. Dante's highest priority right now, and the reason Walter had a job, was diazacol. Nearly a year ago, Favion Pharmaceuticals had given Dr. Dante a large grant to study the effects of its new antidepressant drug on sleep. The lab was testing diazacol on rats, monkeys, and human subjects.

Evelyn was in charge of humans. Her subjects were college boys eager to drop a few pills for $100 a night. Some of them balked at the no-drinking rule—though not for long—and all of them developed a crush on Evelyn. She wasn't really pretty. Her nose was a little too fleshy, her hair a little too limp. Old acne scars roughened her cheeks. But Evelyn was sexy.

Sam was the monkey man. He had been with Dr. Dante for nineteen years. The monkey experiments were twelve-hour-long surgical marathons. The subjects were knocked out, tied down, injected with varying concentrations of diazacol via the femoral artery in their groin, and then "sacrificed." Walter wanted to work on the monkey study until the day he watched Sam scoop the brain out of a dead rhesus monkey with an iced-tea spoon.

As the newest hire and lowest man on the totem pole, Walter was the rat boy. He assisted Dr. Dante during surgery when they implanted tiny steel electrodes into each rat's brain. He injected his four experimental subjects with their daily dose of drug or placebo. He made sure they were fed and watered and that their cages were clean.

Walter hated rats. He was afraid of them. After nine months at the lab he was now allergic to them. Fifteen minutes in their company was enough to cause his nose and eyes to start watering and his face to get all itchy.

During his ten-week-long phase 1 experiment, Walter visited his rats every day. By week three, these daily trips to the animal room had become almost unbearable. It was a dingy, airless warren in the basement of the building where dozens of stainless-steel racks held dozens of stainless-steel cages filled with dozens of purebred white rats.

Crowding was an ongoing challenge for Ivan, the toothless, potbellied gnome who ran the animal room. Researchers always ordered more rats than they needed, a hedge against deaths in transport. The unused rats would languish in the animal room, their bodies bloating, their fur matting, until Ivan finally declared a culling day.

A good culling happened once every three months or so. One day, without warning, Ivan would assemble the unwanted in a large cardboard box near the door and execute them one at a time by grabbing their tails and, with a roundhouse overhand motion akin to swinging an ax, crack their skulls on the edge of the concrete counter.

Walter accidentally wandered into the animal room one day mid-culling. He would never forget the sound of the impact—like an egg cracking, only louder—or the geyser of blood that left a permanent dotted line on the ceiling.

Thank God, Ivan didn't work nights, thought Walter as he grabbed the key to the animal room and jangled it at Evelyn to let her know he was heading downstairs to check on his rats. Ever since Elmer, he'd been extra vigilant.

Walter was feeling cocky about his rat study. The first phase had gone very well. Preliminary results showed that just like humans, rats on diazacol spent less time in deep sleep and more time in REM. "Yes, Walter," joked Evelyn, "rats do dream."

Walter knew that, of course. He had seen the polygraph data. He had also watched Daffy, Porky, Bugs, and Elmer in REM. Their paws and whiskers would twitch. Daffy let out little grunts and whimpers. Bugs lashed his tail so hard that he occasionally knocked the water bottle off the side of his cage.

As he turned down the long hall towards the animal room, Walter remembered a rat study that Evelyn told him about. It was before he came to work at the lab. Dr. Dante had wanted to know how important REM sleep really was to a rat, so he deprived eight rats of REM sleep for four days. Evelyn said that by day three, the rats were so hyper and psychotic they were attacking their cage mates and themselves.

"How did you stop them from dreaming?" Walter had asked.

Evelyn had smiled in obvious appreciation of his question.

"You know how when you go into REM you get super relaxed?" she said. "Muscle tone goes way down? Well, Dante designs this really tippy platform, floats it in the middle of a tub of water, and sits the rats on top. As long as they were awake, they could keep the platform level. As soon as they went into REM, and got all relaxed, the platform tipped, and splooosh. He called it the No Dreaming pool."

"Drowning dreams," whispered Walter. He shuddered as he unlocked the door to the animal room. "Brilliant. Awful."

Walter took a deep breath and held it. Then he pulled the animal room door open. The overhead light came on automatically. Walter felt the warm thickness of menthol and rat piss coat his tongue.

Their cages were across the room, directly ahead of him, second row: DAFFY, PORKY, BUGS written in Walter's neat block lettering on the white index cards taped to their cages. A damaged cable dangled from the handle of Porky's cage. Porky must have chewed through it again. Walter retrieved the cable and retreated to the door, happy with the decision to visit his charges.

Dr. Dante had been pleased with Walter's conscientiousness on the rat study, and impressed by his creative solutions to the niggling problems that regularly plague scientific inquiry. Like the less irritating solvent Walter had developed for diazacol. His three parts albumen to one part lemon juice solution didn't produce open skin sores on the rats the way the hydrochloric acid had. Dr. Dante hadn't even been that upset when Walter told him about Elmer's death.

Walter glanced at the clock on the animal room wall. He'd been in rat country for 90 seconds. He was approaching his breath-holding limit. He stepped back and let the door swing shut. He sprinted halfway down the hallway before stopping to take his first breath at the dead-animal bin, Elmer's final resting place.

Poor Elmer, thought Walter as he spit into the bin. He had been a problem rat from the start. Each afternoon when Walter showed up with his syringes, the other three subjects turned their backs in fear and buried their noses in a corner of the cage. This made it easy for Walter to grab a fingerful of haunch and give it a stick. When Walter opened Elmer's cage, Elmer *backed* into a corner. Then he stared up at Walter, just daring Walter to try and grab a piece of his ass.

Walter had hoped that, like the other rats, Elmer would eventually come to accept his fate, to realize that his life, with Walter as his caretaker, wasn't half bad. Injections aside, Walter pampered his charges. They were well-fed and watered. Their cages were clean. Walter even spent a few minutes each day talking or playing with them. He felt that the stimulation and companionship were good for their overall attitude and health. It was a lab rat's life, to be sure. But it was a good life, an easy life, predictable and secure.

When Walter opened the door to Elmer's cage that Thursday afternoon, Elmer lunged out at him with such force that the electrodes wiring Elmer's head to the panel at the top of his cage came unplugged. Walter managed to sidestep Elmer's airborne body, which sailed past him, plastic-coated wires trailing out behind it, and landed spread-eagle on the linoleum floor about six feet from the cage. Truly, a remarkable leap.

In a blur of fear and self-defense, Walter grabbed the dazed Elmer by the tail and, without hesitating, dropped him into the large glass jar that he used to anesthetize the rats. He emptied a whole bottle of ether in after him and secured the lid.

A few minutes later, as Walter carefully double-bagged Elmer's lifeless body—in compliance with OSHA regulations—he decided that Elmer had been a dreamer. Elmer had dreamed of a life beyond the cage, of something bigger and better. The dream had been his undoing. Cause of death: unrealistic expectations. Walter admired Elmer.

Walter never shared the particulars of Elmer's death. A few days later, Dr. Dante rewarded Walter for his hard work by temporarily reassigning him. In the two-week interim between phase 1 and phase 2 of his rat study, Walter would assist Evelyn with the humans.

Walter headed back up the stairs now, two at a time. He didn't really enjoy working nights, and the idea that he was somehow profiting from Elmer's death made Walter squirm a little, but he liked spending time with Evelyn. She was funny and smart in a practical way. She always told Dr. Dante exactly what was on her mind, the only one in the lab who dared. And Evelyn loved to gossip.

In the week they had been working nights together, Walter learned that Ivan was a retired bus driver whose nagging, hypochondriacal wife might or might not explain why Ivan had French-kissed the lab's last three female interns. He found out that Sam's shriveled left arm was a birth defect, that he'd starting showing up to work with alcohol on his breath after his only son, Sam Jr., came out, and that Leslie, the boss's wife, had been hospitalized twice for depression. Evelyn confirmed that she had indeed slept with Ray, the shaggy blond surfer-dude/post-doc who popped into the lab every now and then. Walter suspected Evelyn and the boss had a thing going too, but she hadn't said anything about that. Not yet, anyway.

Walter used a canister of soldering flux to prop open his paperback copy of *The Fellowship of the Ring*. He finished chapter 7 ("The Mirror of Galadriel") while he rewired Porky's gnawed cable. It was nearly 2 A.M. The whir of the polygraph was making him drowsy.

He looked up at Evelyn. She was sitting at the desk making notes on Mrs. T's chart. Her back was to Walter. The radio was on real low, tuned to the all-night jazz station she liked. Walter glanced over at the polygraph. Mrs. T was sleeping peacefully, hopscotching back and forth between stages 3 and 4.

"When did you start working here? With Dr. Dante?" asked Walter, cutting six-inch lengths of black electrical tape and fastening their ends in a neat row along the edge of the counter.

"Before you were born," said Evelyn.

"Seriously," he said.

Evelyn twirled her chair around to face him.

"Okay. I met Dante at a party, like, twenty years ago. Actually, it'll be twenty-one years next month. It was right before he got engaged to Leslie. We had a few drinks and we got to talking, and he started telling me about this grant he had just gotten to study bats, and he said he was looking for an assistant, and would I be interested in coming to work for him."

"Were you looking for a job?" asked Walter.

"Not really," said Evelyn. "Well, maybe. I was working on a pediatric floor. You know, sick kids." She made a face. "Plus, there's a lot of bullshit in hospitals. Really, you wouldn't believe it. So, bats? Why not?"

"What happened with the bat research anyway?"

"The usual," said Evelyn. "Dante published a paper: "The Bat at Rest: Sleep Architecture of *Myotis lucifugus.*" Or something like that. Then we got our first drug-company grant, and that was the end of the bats. Which I was happy about, because people around here were already starting to call me Robin. Get it?"

Walter got a frisson imagining Evelyn in tights and a cape.

"Do you like your job?" he asked Evelyn, changing the subject. "I mean, do you feel like it was a good decision to quit nursing?"

"Are you writing a book, Walter?"

He laughed.

Evelyn pulled the green plastic Jerry's Bar and Grill ashtray from the desk drawer, a sure sign she was ready to chat. She lit one of the Carlton Lights she'd just started smoking. "Like sucking Jell-O through a cotton ball," she said.

"Do I think it was a good idea to quit nursing?" She repeated the question as she leaned back in her chair and took an intentionally melodramatic drag. "Not financially, it wasn't. I could have made a lot more money as a nurse, especially if I'd been willing to work nights and maybe pull a double every now and then. I probably would have helped more people, too. You know, contributed more to society?"

She paused long enough to lick a spot of yogurt off the Y on her YMCA sweatshirt.

"This job is a lot less stressful than nursing, though, so I'll probably live longer," she continued. "It's more flexible, too, so I can spend more time with my kid. It's really hard to answer that question, Walter. I'm sure I would have been happy and miserable in either job. In both jobs. Just for different reasons."

"So, you don't think there's, like, *one* career that was meant for you?" he asked.

"Okay, Walter, back to work," said Evelyn, swinging her chair around. "You know how I hate that woo-woo crap."

This was another thing Walter liked about Evelyn, envied really. She didn't second-guess. She didn't believe in regrets or in destiny. She didn't feel sorry for herself. She just kept moving forward.

Walter assumed their conversation was over. He wrapped the last strip of tape around the cable and coated the tape job with clear nail polish to deter any future chewing. A moment later, Evelyn swung back around.

"Are you Catholic, Walter?" she said, leaning forward in the chair.

"I was raised Catholic, but I'm—"

"I knew it!" said Evelyn. She reached back and pounded her cigarette into the ashtray.

"Here's a flash, Walter. All that stuff about God having a plan? A plan for you, a plan for me, a plan for the world? It's bullshit! Look at Mrs. T in there. You think nightmares are part of some plan God has for her? I tell you what, if I had to schlep Stouffer's frozen macaroni and cheese all day, I'd be having nightmares, too!"

Evelyn finished off her second Diet Pepsi. She lit another cigarette. She cast a quick glance in the direction of the polygraphs.

"You know what?" she went on. "You can decide to be a doctor, or you can pump gas. God could care less. *If* there even is a God, which is a whole 'nother conversation." She was waving her cigarette back and forth in the air between them now. "Whatever you do, you'll be happy, unhappy, frustrated, insecure. All if it. Guaranteed. So, stop agonizing. And stop waiting around for some burning bush to tell you what you should do and who you should be."

At 4:15 A.M., Walter decided to make coffee. Mrs. T was deep into stage 4. Evelyn was napping on the cot, wrapped up in the sleeping bag, probably enjoying a light stage 2 slumber. He watched her for a while. He tried to imagine himself twenty years from now. Would that be him, dozing on the cot?

Walter could picture himself staying at the lab, working his way through graduate school. Master's degree, PhD, post-doc. The sleep stuff was fascinating, no doubt about it. In nine or ten years, he'd have his own research program, his own lab, his own assistants. He'd ride to work on a vintage Norton. He'd only wear ties to deliver groundbreaking papers at major scientific conferences. He could see the path before him. It was a good path, challenging, respectable, and attainable.

Walter warmed his hands on either side of the Mr. Coffee machine and watched with satisfaction as the steamy brew's dark meniscus crept past the four-cup line on the Pyrex pot.

At first, he thought it was the zipper. He thought that Evelyn had yanked open the sleeping bag's zipper quickly and with force. But when he turned and looked down at Evelyn, she hadn't stirred. Then the pens swerved again, wildly. Suddenly they were mad, careening back and forth across the paper like the flailing arms of a shipwrecked man. Before Walter could move, the gray door burst open. It crashed against the desk with a metallic clang, and Mrs. T came flying through it, her white nightgown pressed against her breasts and thighs, a tangle of long brown hair and red and green electrodes streaming behind her. She shot across the darkened lab, a ghostly blur, and came to rest at the far side, clutching the counter and retching into the sink.

Walter reached her first. He rested his hands against her arms and gently turned her around. Her nightgown was damp with sweat. Her eyes were wide, pupils dilated. She didn't see Walter. She was still in the dream.

Walter could feel the terror. It radiated from Mrs. T like heat. He spread his feet further apart and bent his knees, bracing himself for whatever might happen when she finally woke up. Walter had nightmares. His worst was the one where his car skidded off a bridge at night and plunged into a cold, black river. He woke up choking with his palms pressed against the wall next to his bed.

When Mrs. T came around, she went limp against Walter. Once she described her nightmare—something about her daughter and a collapsing igloo—it was easy to get her back to sleep. Evelyn detached the electrodes and helped her into the bed. She left the gray door ajar.

"My God," whispered Evelyn. She was bending over the polygraph. She had turned off the paper feed and was rifling through the record of Mrs. T's nightmare. "She wasn't even in REM yet, Walter. Look."

Evelyn stopped at the page where Mrs. T's nightmare began. She traced the jagged pen etchings with her fingertips. "A&P must be worse than I thought."

Two months later, Dr. Dante got a handwritten note from Mrs. T. He posted it on the corkboard near the coffee machine. Apparently, her neurologist had taken Dr. Dante's advice and put Mrs. T on amoxidine, a deep-sleep suppressor. Mrs. T was still having the night terrors. But they seemed to occur less frequently now, and she felt the psychotherapy was helping her cope with their intensity. The therapist had been encouraging her to write a book about her experience.

Walter read the letter while he waited for the fresh pot to brew. He generally avoided caffeine this late in the afternoon, but it had been a long week. He was back on days now, finishing up with a new roster of rats. He missed working with Evelyn. He'd been getting to work a little earlier so he could catch her before she left for home. She seemed a little distracted these days. Walter noticed dark roots in her blonde hair.

He removed Mrs. T's note from the bulletin board and slipped it into the embryology section of his anatomy book. Then he scrubbed and rinsed the last rat cage and placed it on the stainless-steel cart with the others. He'd wheel them down to the animal room on his way out. Walter filled his mug with coffee, poured in what he guessed was about three teaspoons of sugar, and sat down at the desk to finish up some paperwork.

He made one final addition to the list of his duties that Dr. Dante had asked him to prepare. He typed out a copy of his formula for the diazacol solvent, adding a few footnotes on preparation at the bottom. He rummaged through the desk drawer until he found the Polaroid that he took of Evelyn sitting on one of the sleep chamber beds with a full set of electrodes taped to her face. She had made Walter practice on her before she'd let him wire up his first subject.

"You have a nice touch, Walter." That's what she said when he'd finished.

Walter slipped the photo in his back pocket. He scribbled a note for Evelyn, folded it in half, then in half again. On his way out, he taped it to the front of the polygraph.

E-

Thanks for everything. My mother will forward any mail. Sweet dreams.

W.

PS: You need coffee.

DANCING WITH THE DEVIL

Lucy Pond

I was ten years old the day Mom came home with news that she had landed not just one job, but two. Normally sober and withdrawn, she burst through the door that day with an ear-to-ear grin like I'd never seen on her. She was glowing. She'd been to a beauty parlor. Her fine brown hair was curled into soft finger waves. She even wore light red lipstick and makeup.

With a satisfied flourish, she announced, "This is the best day of our lives!" She set her purse on the pine hope chest we used as a sofa and took off her nice gray jacket, the one that usually hung in the back of her closet. "Our luck is turning around," she announced. "I found a rental house today. It's small, but has a big yard." She grinned as if she'd seen a vision, barely able to control her excitement. "We're leaving the projects! No more public assistance."

Our dad, Eddie, closed his paperback and looked up from the kitchen table. Suprised, he took a slow drag from his cigarette and brushed ashes off his white T-shirt.

Louise, my bossy older sister—fourteen going on forty—put down her library book. She was goggle-eyed. I was, too.

My younger brothers, Buddy and Scooter, stopped wrestling and sat up.

"Everyone is going to have work harder," Mom said, looking at Dad. "I can't do it by myself."

I ran over and grabbed her hand. "I'll pack," I said, a convert to her cause. "I'll clean. I'll watch the boys. You can count on me, I promise." I followed her into the kitchen and grabbed the broom, proving my good intentions. But Mom didn't see me. She was glassy-eyed, seeing in the distance a Better Life.

Dad flashed Mom a hopeful grin. "Well," he said. "I'm not helpless, you know." He refilled the blue enamel teakettle and turned on the stove. "I've been looking for a job and now I'll try harder." Mom gave him a wary look. She'd heard that promise before.

"I found a waitress job at the Terry Café," Mom continued in high gear. "It's right across the street from the Yellow Cab Company."

"Sounds great," Dad grunted, filling his cup with hot water and pouring a cup for her. "Cabbies are the best tippers." Reaching for the Folgers, his eyes bulged. I practically saw a thought pop into his brain. "Hey, maybe I can get a job driving a cab," he said.

"The extra money from the Terry will help buy furniture and get us settled," Mom said, ignoring Dad's plea for attention. "We're set."

"If that's what you want . . . two jobs," Dad said. "I thought you got paid for the summer with your teaching job."

"I do," Mom countered. "But this is extra money we'll need

to get going." She stirred her coffee and stared at the stack of dirty breakfast dishes.

"Maybe I can buy some new school clothes," Louise sighed.

I didn't say anything.

It was June 1958. The new house was in the very south end of Seattle, a forgotten part of the city—east of Boeing Field, south of Rainier Beach, and north of Renton. Nowhere. As a neighborhood, it didn't even rate a name. It was home to white families on the very first rung of the economic ladder, but to me it looked like paradise.

Our new house was odd looking—one story with an unfinished basement—but no one complained. The outside was fake brick that didn't fool anyone. Inside, the narrow living room fed into a tiny kitchen. There were three bedrooms: one for Mom and Dad, one for the boys, and one for the girls. One bathroom.

Mom said she would pay two dollars to anyone who helped paint. Louise and I couldn't start fast enough. We were working for movie money! For twenty-five cents we could see two movies and one newsreel at the Beacon Hill Theater.

The day we moved in, I wore a blue cotton blouse, pink shorts, and my favorite blue Keds. I sat on a tree stump in our brambly back yard and arched my skinny ten-year-old spine, posing like a movie star. I was Scarlett O'Hara returning to Tara. I looked at our house and wondered if the servants had stayed on.

"Loretta!" Louise screamed from the window. "Stop daydreaming and get up here and help! Now!" There was fury in her beady brown eyes.

"I'm taking a break," I shouted. "I'll be there in a sec." We'd never had a yard before and I loved looking at it. But Miss Bossy Pants came running down the back stairs after me. She wagged her finger in my face and hissed, "Put your stuff in your half of the bedroom, then help unpack the kitchen. And where are the boys? Find them!"

"Where's Dad?" I complained. "He should be watching the boys."

"He left hours ago," she said, distractedly.

In the living room, surrounded by boxes, Louise was trying to unpack. "How are we going to get this done?" I asked. "Dad should be here." I carried a box and a shopping bag of clothes to my room. When I returned I told Louise, "I'm telling Mom that Dad didn't help."

Louise said matter-of-factly, "Forget it. Mom will make excuses for him like she always does. It doesn't matter."

"It does matter," I cried. "He's supposed to be watching us. He never helps. Why can't Mom be here? He should be at work, and she should be home with us." I marched back to my room yelling back to Louise, "Dad ruins everything. I hate him."

Just then I saw a blur out the window. It was Buddy running down the street and Scooter vainly trying to keep up with him. Scooter, barely more than a toddler, carrying his favorite yellow blankey.

"You boys need to come in." I screamed from the porch.

In the house, Buddy, the bully, was laughing like a maniac, and Scooter was crying. I got Scooter into the bathroom and began washing him. I yelled at Buddy, who was Dad's pet, "You're a brat and no one likes you."

A moment later, Dad's car pulled into the driveway.

Dad called to us from the living room. "You kids come in here and sit down. I'll be right back." A few minutes later he returned with a black dog on a leash. "Kids—meet Cindy. What do you think? Is she a beauty or what?" Cindy was a full-grown, shaggy, black dog. She wagged her tail and panted with excitement. We ran over and showered her with kisses.

"I walked into the pound and looked in all the cages," Dad said, giving Cindy little pats on the behind. "I stopped when I saw this girl. I knew right away she was our dog." Dad smiled and hand-combed his hair. He was proud of himself.

I had to admit sometimes he did get it right.

For the first couple of weeks in the new house Dad was on his best behavior. Then, slowly, he found other dads in the neighborhood who shared his passions—beer, baseball, and the Saturday-night fights. He wanted to get Buddy playing ball as soon as possible, but he wasn't impressed with the local team. "These boys play baseball like sissies," he groaned. "I'm surprised they don't wear skirts." Dad had had a brief flirtation with minor league baseball, so his offer to coach was snapped up. He was excited by his new position of authority and threw himself into the task. Here was a chance to spend time with his two loves: Buddy and baseball. He would groom Buddy to be the team's ace pitcher.

Throughout the summer Louise continued to be the crabby adult-in-training. With Mom working so much and Dad busy with baseball and general idleness, she was left to take care of us kids and the house. In spite of my promises to Mom, I didn't cook or clean or watch my brothers. Buddy and Scooter were wild—always fighting and causing trouble. Dad never did his share. Mom was never home. I resisted Louise's bossiness, which meant leaving the house early and coming back late. I hated doing chores.

Cindy and I liked walking around the neighborhood and talking with whomever we found at home. About a block from our house was the Croker's cream-colored frame house. It had two stories and a nice front yard, a very nice house for this neighborhood. Pastor and Mrs. Croker happened to be in the yard when we strolled by. Pastor Croker was a slight man who seldom smiled. I'd seen him before at Bob's Market. He had lank blond hair, and his small blue eyes flickered between sternness and worry. His hands were delicate, like a woman's.

Sue Croker wore a yellow and white summer print dress

with white, high-heeled shoes. She looked like June Cleaver. I felt more comfortable with her than the pastor. "Loretta," she cooed, "won't you come in and have a glass of lemonade with us?" I didn't hesitate for a second.

Inside, the three of us sat at their large, oak dining room table.

"Do you go to a church, Loretta?" Pastor Croker asked, looking intently at me.

I couldn't answer. The lemonade was the sourest drink I'd ever had—just lemons and water. I wanted to spit it out, but I couldn't. After a big nasty swallow, I answered.

"I've gone to church before," I gasped, "but in our old neighborhood."

"We have a lovely church at the top of the hill, Loretta," the pastor said. "I hope you will come and worship with us." He invited me to come to their church any Sunday morning at 10 A.M. and told me how to get there. "And Loretta—bring your whole family."

"Okay," I said, but I was sure no one in my family would be interested.

"Have you ever gone to a revival?" Sue asked. I shook my head no.

Sue smiled and held my hand. "They are amazing." Her eyes got big and her round face even more welcoming. "Many, many people come together, and we welcome Christ to join us. When people feel Jesus touch them, they step forward and accept Christ as their savior. There's singing and clapping, and soon Jesus is right in the tent with us."

I had no idea what she was talking about, but I liked the idea of being invited to a place where Jesus would show up. "Do you mean Jesus comes to your meetings?" I was taken aback.

"Yes, dear," Sue beamed. "He's always at our services."

I was thrilled. "Oh crumb, I can't wait."

At first I didn't like the pastor, but after a few visits I realized he was just serious, like Mom. Pastor Croker and Sue were endlessly curious about my family. "Does your Dad have a job?" Sue asked. "He always seems to be home."

"Yep," I said. "He's home. He's putting together a Little League team."

They looked worried. "And your mother—we hardly ever see her. What kind of work does she do?"

"She's a teacher and a waitress. But school doesn't start until September, so she's working lots of extra shifts at the restaurant. She's making sure we never go on welfare again." I was proud of how hard my Mom worked and hoped they would be, too. But without any comment Sue continued, "Don't you have a baby-sitter? You kids are so young."

"That's Louise's job," I explained. "She's fourteen. And Dad's home most of the time."

I wanted out of their scrutiny, so I asked about Jesus, and they were pretty quick to change track onto the Son of God and Blessed Savior business. I already knew that. What I really wanted to know about was the Devil. He was a true magician, jumping in and out of people, making them do horrible things.

The Crokers talked about Heaven and Hell as if there was a big decision about which place was best. Any fool would choose Heaven, I knew, but I suspected they thought my family and I were on the fast track to Hell. I wanted a chance to prove them wrong.

Sue broke my reverie. "Loretta, dear," she said, "have you been saved?" I wasn't sure what she was talking about.

"Probably not," I admitted.

I skipped the whole way home. I'd never been around anyone who talked so much about people we couldn't see. It was fun listening to the Crokers.

Two afternoons later, when the Crokers weren't home, I stopped to talk to Mrs. Parks, who lived next door to them. I met her the first day we moved in and immediately liked her.

She must have felt the same since she invited me to come over anytime I wanted. When I knocked on her back door, she was doing her chores, as always, but she asked me in.

Mrs. Parks continued ironing and I sat at her kitchen table eating a cupcake and drinking a big glass of cold milk. I asked her why she didn't go to the Crokers' church, since she lived right next door to them.

"I'm not the one to ask about the Crokers, dear," she said. "I've never had a conversation with either of them." She paused and looked at me. "To tell you the truth, Loretta, I think they're stuck up. They think they're better than the rest of us."

I wet my pointer finger and picked the crumbs off my plate.

Mrs. Parks sighed as she hung a freshly ironed shirt on a clothes hanger. "I've seen you over at their house," she said. "I'm sure they're nice to you. Are they trying to get you to go their church?"

I said that the Crokers were very nice indeed and had invited me to their church.

Mrs. Parks sat down at the table and looked me in the eye. "Honey," she said, "it's none of my business, but I'm not sure you should get involved with them."

"What do you mean?" I asked.

She said, "People say they're a bunch of kooks at that church!"

It was clear that Mrs. Parks didn't understand the Crokers, but I liked her anyway. "I have to go," I said. "Thanks a lot for the cupcake and milk!"

Later, as I was helping Mom fold clothes, I mentioned meeting the pastor and his wife. "I'd like to go their church sometime," I said. "Would you come with me?" I hadn't been alone with Mom since we were school shopping at the Goodwill. Mom's long fingers hand-pressed each article of clothing. She made a fresh pile for each of us. Even though Louise worked hard to keep our lives in order, our house was messy, so Mom's crisply folded laundry looked like soft sculptures in a sea of chaos. "I'm not saying I won't," Mom said, "but I don't know when."

I persisted. "Well, what do you think about me going to their church alone, then?"

"That's fine, dear," Mom said, "but you'll have to walk."

The following Sunday morning, I woke up early, very excited. I pulled on my blue jeans and pink T-shirt and didn't stop to comb my hair. Without waking anyone, Cindy and I slipped out the front door, walked straight up the steep hill, about a mile from our house, then turned left at the water tower, just like Pastor Croker had said. After a few turns we came around a corner and there it was—a small white church with a thin, elegant steeple. It was simple and beautiful. I'd seen churches like this in the movies. It seemed like I'd been there a thousand times.

Cindy and I watched the people get out of their cars and walk up the wooden steps to the church. Pastor Croker, wearing a black robe, shook hands with everyone as they entered. And he was smiling!—something I hadn't seen before. Cindy and I sat outside on the steps and listened. We could hear it all—the sermon and the singing. It was magical! I loved hearing the hands clapping and feet stomping, the shouted "Amens." This—the pastor and the congregation, the energy—felt like family.

After the service, when everyone had left, Pastor Croker saw me and called me over. "I'm glad you made it, Loretta. But why didn't you come in?" I looked down at my clothes.

"It doesn't matter what clothes you wear in the House of the Lord," he said. "We are all equal in God's eyes."

I smiled.

"Loretta, I've been meaning to ask, are you interested in doing the Lord's work?"

"Oh, yes," I said quickly, "I'd like that very much."

I had just accepted my first real job. When I got home, I announced that I now worked for the Lord. I guess no one believed me because no one said anything. I went to my room and wrote out some questions for Pastor Croker. I needed more details about my job.

Church was exciting. I accepted Christ as my savior right away. This meant I had to start saving others, but first I had some catching up to do. I started going to church most nights of the week. There was prayer group, bible study, Pioneer Girls, and choir practice. And on Saturday nights, I went with the church down to Tacoma for Youth for Christ. It was grand. I loved these people, and they cared about me. I was Sister Loretta.

I made a commitment to do the Lord's work—all the time. Quick learner that I was, it didn't take long to understand the vocabulary. The name for everyone who wasn't saved was Sinner. Acts against God or the church were Sins. Forgiveness is what's required once a Sin has been committed. The place Sinners were heading was Hell. It was full of pain and suffering. All good people are Saved. All of the rules of Salvation are mapped out in the Bible. The Bible is always right. And there was a trickster named the Devil who tried to lure people to hell. The Devil could not be underestimated. He was powerful and meant business. He had once been an angel in Heaven but got kicked out. The Devil was in a constant battle with Jesus over who went where when they died. He had it easy over at my house.

The list of how the Devil made his way into one's life was long. These activities became forbidden: Movies. Dancing. Rock 'n' roll music. Television. Drinking. Smoking. Stealing. Swearing. Showing off. Bragging. Wearing makeup. Wearing tight clothes. Sex with anyone other than your marriage partner. Taking the Lord's name in vain. Cheating. Lying. Disobeying your parents. Not going to church. Wearing patent-leather shoes. And all the other stuff you know you aren't supposed to do.

The hardest thing for me to give up was the movies. It was our most special treat. I didn't want to give this up, but my life wasn't my own any more. I worked for the Lord now.

Back home I had a new role in the family: Devil-lookout. I took it upon myself to spy on everyone. I knew I would have no trouble spotting the Devil. Mom was the only member of our family, other than me, who I figured had a chance at Heaven. I couldn't find anything to qualify Mom as a Sinner. But I was going to be busy with everyone else.

When I had time, I'd lie under Louise's bed, knowing it wouldn't be long before the Devil would take charge. I'd seen her turn on a rock 'n' roll radio station and dance in the mirror. Or try on different types of makeup. Or make plans to sneak out with friends.

Once I got more than I bargained for. I was lying under her bed listening to her end of a phone conversation. "I don't know about this new house," she said. "Some of the neighbors are creepy. There's an old man living next door—he's at least forty. I haven't caught him yet, but I think he stands outside our bedroom window." She took a deep breath, "I've noticed the grass is flattened only next to our window and there's a well-worn path to the back door of his house." She caught her breath and whispered, "I think he watches Loretta and me undress."

I gasped and almost inhaled a dust ball. Louise jumped off the bed and screamed: "Come out of there, you little creep. I'm going to kill you." She tried to grab my arm, but I escaped out the other side of the bed.

"Why are you mad at me?" I yelled at her. "We have to tell Dad about Mr. Bates. The Devil must be inside of him." But Louise was furious.

I locked myself in the bathroom to keep her from hitting me. "I want to take you to Heaven with me," I shouted. "God only loves those who are devoted to him. I don't want you to go to Hell."

"I'm sick of you spying on me," she yelled and banged the door. She didn't see that I was trying to help her. "I'm sick of Jesus," she said. "I'm sick of you!"

At Bible study we read passages from the Good Book. "Be sober, be vigilant, because your adversary the Devil, as a roaring lion, walketh about, seeking who he may devour." I raised my hand and asked why the Lord wasn't strong enough to bring everyone to Heaven. It sounded to me like the Devil was working harder than Jesus. Sue reminded me that we are born as sinners. Earth isn't the Promised Land. It is where we have the opportunity to cleanse our souls so we can sit with Jesus in Heaven. Soon the lights were turned out and we were looking at slides of people in Africa—Black people with no clothes on. The Pastor asked if I thought these people looked like Christians. "Would a Christian woman walk around without being fully covered?" he asked. "No. The Devil is in these people unless we can get there and save them."

I began dreaming of going to Africa and saving lost souls. In church we saw pictures of the heathens—millions of them. I loved their faces. They didn't know any better. I couldn't understand why these people were sent to Hell just because we didn't get there in time. It didn't seem fair. I had work to do. But first I had the home front to deal with: the Devil visiting the old man next door. I lay awake at night trying to think how I might catch him in the act.

When Dad heard about me spying on Louise he hit the roof. He found me out front watering the grass.

"Loretta, I don't want you bothering Louise anymore. Is that clear?"

"You like Louise more than me," I complained. "You always take her side."

"Hey, Carrot." Dad stood over me. "I like you plenty, but Louise works harder than you. She's the prettiest and the smartest, and you're probably jealous, but that's just the way it is."

I screamed at him, "I'm not jealous of her, but what's left for me?"

"You are missing the point, Loretta. I don't want you bothering Louise."

He was wrong. They both were wrong. "Why should I agree to let Louise go to Hell? I'm not giving up on her. Besides, if I wasn't spying on her, I wouldn't have found out about Mr. Bates watching us undress."

He stopped short, as if I'd hit him. "What are you talking about?"

"Ask Louise. He stands outside our bedroom window when it's dark."

Dad stuck his hands in his pockets and twisted them from side to side, which hiked up his khakis two or three inches. "Loretta," he said, "that's a terrible thing you just said. Wait here while I get to the bottom of this. For your sake, I hope you aren't lying."

Later I saw Dad pounding on Mr. Bates' front door. Dad's face was red and he was yelling, "I'll smash your head in with this baseball bat if I ever see you near my house or my daughters again!" Mr. Bates didn't even open his door.

Dad told me Mom was gone so much because she hated my "Jesus crap," as he called it. "That's not true," I shouted. "She's gone because someone has to work to make money. Why don't you get a job? Or just leave. You are always causing problems." I hated to cry in front of him, so I held my tears and ran into my room. He knew I liked Mom more than him, and he was trying to hurt my feelings. Besides, he liked staying home and drinking. And he knew that I knew. I was impressed by how he handled Mr. Bates, but he was still bound for Hell.

My brothers were heathens and might as well have been born in Africa. There wasn't anything I could do about them. Dad wanted me to take them to church with me, but that was just because he didn't want to look after them. I tried to think of ways to save them, but it was a lost cause. So when it came to my brothers, I did what I could. I pretended they didn't exist.

Louise was the one I thought I might be able to save. She had her faults, but it didn't seem like she had to be a Sinner. Sometimes, though, when she was sweeping and thought no one was home she would dance with the broom. One day I saw her turn up the radio—Buddy Holly was singing "Everyday"—

and she got that faraway look. Usually Louise looked angry, but at that moment, dancing with the broom, she looked really pretty. Still, I had to save her. She was dancing with the Devil! I got a glass of cold water and threw it on her. With water dripping down her face, she screamed and began swinging the broom at me. I ran out the door as fast as I could. She was furious, but at least I'd chased the Devil away.

When Mom came home I looked over her shoulder while she worked on a crossword. She didn't like to be interrupted, but that didn't stop me. I pleaded, "Will you comb my hair? I can't get the snarls out of the back." She tapped her pen, thinking about a clue. She couldn't hear me.

"Can you come to church this Sunday to hear me sing?" I asked. "Do you want to come downtown to the Y and see me swim? We could take the bus together."

I resorted to gossip: "Buddy cheats at checkers and hides Scooter's toys and makes him cry." Still no response.

I whispered in her ear: "Scooter pees in back of the toilet— on purpose."

"Dad laughs a lot when you aren't here."

When Mom finished the puzzle, she looked at me as if I had just entered the room. She hadn't heard anything I said.

"Why do you stay with Dad?" I asked her. "He isn't really sick, and he doesn't help our family. If he worked, you could be home more."

Mom ignored my question. She said softly, "Queenie"— that was her name for me—"I don't worry about you. I know you're all right, and that's a comfort."

I was never curious about Mom's puzzles. I knew they were for smart people, and I wasn't smart, so I left them alone. But Dad's books got my attention. I knew I shouldn't open them, but one way the Devil kept a foothold in our family was through that filth and I needed to find out what was in them. I was intrigued by the titles: *Roadside Night: The Strange Love of Those Who Dared. Born Innocent: Behind the Walls of a Girls Reformatory. The Sex Test. Johnny Bogan: A Realistic Novel of Violent Young Love.*

Sitting in the living room one day, I put a few of Dad's books inside my Bible to conceal them. I flipped through the pages. "I wear short nighties and heat up fast," one of the girls said. Another warned: "I'm going to do something about you, big boy. Right now." Men "had their way" with delinquent girls who escaped from reform school. The girls had "flesh so hot I could light matches on them." Then there was Skippy, the young boy with the body of a man. "Skippy's loins ached with that familiar longing as he watched Aunt Joan sit naked at her dresser, her luxuriant breasts swaying as she combed her auburn hair."

As I read I noticed a tickle deep inside my body. I'd never felt that before, but knew right away it was bad. I sat up straight, put Dad's books back and walked off with my Bible, breathing hard. I ran outside and congratulated myself on winning another battle over the Devil.

At church I'd become Pastor Croker's favorite. On Sundays the service began at 10 A.M., but I got there at 9 and made sure the hymnals were placed upright on the back of each pew. I swept and generally got the church looking clean, and then I sat in the front row when the service began. The pastor's voice soared with spirit. "Help us, O God, on our journey. We sinners get lost easily in the sea of temptation. Your word will guide us. Your love will give us courage to fight the Devil. Without your guiding light we are damned to an eternity of fire." He lifted his arms when he spoke, which in his robe made him look about three times his size. "We are not worthy of your love, O Lord, yet we beg your assistance. Evil lurks in the hearts of each and every one of us. We tremble with weakness. Make us strong."

"Amen," we answered.

"Each one of us has sinned through our thoughts, those things we have done, and those we have failed to do. We humbly ask your forgiveness."

"Amen."

Now the pastor bellowed powerfully, "We must change and

become like little children. Let us pray together." And the entire congregation stood and sang "Holy, Holy, Holy."

At home I avoided contact with anyone in my family except Mom. I'd given up. They were goners and there was nothing I could do. I liked to sit in my bedroom and study certain passages from the Bible. "Be of good cheer, I have overcome the world." Why would Jesus say this and still say that everyone who is not saved is going to Hell? If Jesus has overcome the world, wouldn't that mean he was stronger than the Devil? The Bible was becoming less clear to me than it was in the beginning.

Pastor Croker stopped me after Bible study one day. "Loretta, you are ready for your own class of students. Would you like to teach?"

I was stunned and complimented—and scared. "Yes," I stammered. "Sure."

I enjoyed working with the younger children. We colored pictures that corresponded to Bible stories. Teaching helped me understand the Bible more and also showed me that there was a lot of room for interpretation of these stories.

For the next three years, I was completely devoted to our pastor and our church. But when I entered junior high school I quickly found two girls, Diane and Susan, whom I liked a lot and who wanted to be my best friends. I didn't ask, but I was sure neither of them was Christian. I knew they didn't go to church, and I didn't even want to know if they'd accepted Christ as their Savior. I just knew that I liked them, and they didn't feel like sinners. We had fun together.

I began to cut back on the amount of time I devoted to the church. Fortunately I was getting a little old for Pioneer Girls. I told Linda Grant, our leader, "I'm too busy with school now. I need to do homework after school, and I can't promise I'll be coming anymore." Linda smiled and gave me a hug. "Come when you can, Loretta. You are the cornerstone of our Pioneer Girl group. It won't be the same without you."

I also pulled away from choir. More and more I wanted to

be with my new friends, and my church commitments were getting in the way.

In school we started to have dances and, of course, I didn't go. It wasn't an option for a good Christian. But I was curious. I had never wanted to dance, so it wasn't hard to give up, but Diane and Susan went to the dances and loved them. They told me who they danced with, who looked stupid, and who wore what. I was missing something and I knew it.

The church was a wedge between my new friends and me, and I struggled to keep active in both sides of my life. I couldn't talk to Pastor Croker or Sue about my growing doubt about the church and where it fit into my new life. I knew they would say I was being tempted by the Devil and that I should hold firm in my convictions.

I decided to talk with God myself, which I did at night after my prayers. "Dear God, I love you. I know your way is the right way, but I want to listen to music and learn to dance. I know it's not the Devil talking through me. I've been a devoted servant. Are you testing me?"

I cried as I waited for an answer, but none came. For the first time since I became a Christian, I felt doubt. Again I turned to Jesus and pleaded, "Why are you doing this to me?" Still, no answer.

To make matters worse, I was also losing my discipline for avoiding the movies. I wished I could go again.

At school, Diane announced that she was having a slumber party on the following Saturday. "You just have to come, Loretta," she said. "You keep missing everything that's fun. If you want to be my friend, you have to come!" I was stunned. She was daring me. Friendship or exile.

"I'll be there," I said, "unless I have to be home to watch my brothers."

We hugged. "Good. Susan is going to teach us some new

dance steps from *American Bandstand*. It's going to be sooo much fun."

I was petrified. I'd never danced. I'd never seen *American Bandstand*. They were going to find out about me.

That night, before sleep, I stared at my picture of Jesus. I knew He was there when we needed him. That's what I told my Sunday school class and that's what I believed. But almost a week had passed, and I had heard nothing from Jesus. I decided to flip a coin three times. Two out of three came up heads. Finally, a real answer. I was going to the slumber party. I knew God was with me. If I shouldn't go, I would have got tails, but they came up heads!

Two weeks later, before Sunday services, I was sweeping the chapel when a shadow fell over me. It was Pastor Croker. I looked up, happy to see him, but saw he was angry. I stood still as a statue. His arms were folded across his chest, his mouth a flat, tight line. He wasted no time. "Loretta, have you been dancing?" He knew the answer.

I looked up at him, wanting to lie, but I didn't. "Yes," I said.

The pastor's eyes became beady, and his face bloomed an angry pink. I had never seen him like this. "Not you!" he spat. "I never thought this would happen to you. When I heard the Devil was inside of you and that you were making a fool of yourself in front of others, I couldn't believe it."

He put his hands on my shoulders. "Loretta, I wish this wasn't so, but now I know it is." He took the broom away. "Have you asked Jesus for His forgiveness?"

"No," I said. I backed away from him. I had to say something. "I didn't do anything wrong," I cried. "I did dance, it's true, but it didn't have anything to do with the Devil. Honest! I still love Jesus, and I still want to work for the Lord. Nothing's changed!"

"You can't do both, Loretta." Suddenly Pastor Croker looked more like the Devil than one of God's ministers. In his nearer-to-God voice he ordered, "Go home, Loretta, and choose. You need to pray for Jesus' forgiveness. It's out of my hands. Do not come back until you are ready to live like a true Christian."

I walked out the door, crying. I was humiliated. When I got to the bottom of the steps the pastor called after me: "Loretta?" I turned around hoping he'd changed his mind.

"I've never been so disappointed in anyone."

I ran home crying the whole way. I was still me. I still loved the Lord, but Pastor Croker couldn't see that. He didn't understand. I didn't want to give up dancing. I didn't want to lose Susan and Diane. I knew my new friends weren't sinners. He had it wrong.

Friday night at dinner, Louise asked why I was missing choir practice.

"I just don't want to go," I said. I wasn't ready to admit that I'd been asked to leave the church.

Louise was surprised, "Aren't you afraid you're losing some of your Jesus points?"

I ignored her. It was none of her business.

After dinner we cleared the dishes, and I went to the pantry to get the broom.

DISTINCT AND DIFFERENT

Erika Teschke

It was mid-June in Ohio, a high cookie-consumption period. Lots of picnics and parties with neighbors trying to impress one another by serving fancy bagged cookies.

Mattie had returned home that summer from college and needed a job. Fireside Farm brought on extra hands in their Midnight Delight factory during the summer months. Mattie had never worked in a factory, but her distaste for most things privileged put factory work high on her list of things she must do. Born to a mother with a huge inheritance and a father who bought and sold that money for a living, Mattie knew all about plaid uniforms, ponies, and the power that comes with growing up privileged. She hated it all.

Mattie interviewed with Jack, a middle-aged white guy who lifted one side of his lip when he spoke. On the wall of the office, in a frame that said "#1 Pooch," he had a picture of his dachshund. He wore expensive shoes. He looked her up and down, lingering where her sundress ended and her bare legs began, set her wages at $5.30 per hour, and gave her the rundown. "You wear the hairnet we give you, you got me? I don't want no long black hippie hair in the batter. We supply you with two aprons and any safety equipment that is required by OSHA. Other than that, you're on your own. I don't want you showing up here in crusty clothes and smelling like ass. And none of those things you got on. Get some real shoes that cover your painted-up toes. No drinking, no drugs, and no complaining. You don't like it here, go work at 7-Eleven, if you think they'd have you. You got that?"

It seemed as straightforward as she expected it would be: no frills, just plain and simple. The smell of baking cookies permeated his office. Mattie was anxious to get to work.

According to her mother, Mattie had been a difficult and demanding child from the start. She was stubborn and lacked some basic talents. She never learned how to ride a bike and permanently scarred both knees trying. For six months straight she careened herky-jerky down the hill in front of the house with her jaw clenched and her arms unbending. Her mother stood out of view on the porch and smoked cigarettes.

After high school, Mattie went off to an exclusive women's college. She pleased her parents and herself by majoring in political science and minoring in social work. So when she announced to her mother that she was going to work at Fireside, the response was as expected. "*Mattie.* You *can't* be serious. You will be bored in an instant." Her mother leaned one hip against the kitchen counter and gently palpated the back of her recently coiffed hair. She had a batch of hot cross buns in the oven. Her wedding ring—which Mattie referred to as "the house on the hand" because it cost more than most single family dwellings—flashed the Morse code of the rich. She prattled on about Mattie's lack of vision and past mistakes, like giving money to the Christian Children's Fund, something she always brought up. She finished her diatribe with a comment about "those" people in factories and how they get their arms ripped off.

"It's not a baking factory," Mattie said. "It's a place where 'Heartfelt Cookies' are created." She took a running start, slid across the hardwood floor to the walk-in pantry and pulled out her mother's secret stash of Midnight Delights. These were the only sweets her overly disciplined mother allowed herself (she wouldn't touch her own creations) and only then to be eaten out of the sight of others.

"Even you can't resist the pull of the decadent dessert." Mattie swung around, taunting her mother with her pinkies held high, and read in an English accent from the back of the bag:

> "Once you've had your first warming taste of Fireside Farm Heartfelt Cookies, no other snack will do. They are not just crunchy goodness, they are a delectable combination of pure, wholesome ingredients and fond memories, reminding us of simpler, easier times. So curl up, grant yourself a favor, and indulge tonight in Fireside Farms' Midnight Delights. You'll find yourself savoring the moment."

The sun came through the kitchen window and reflected off the stainless-steel appliances. Her mother squinted. Mattie tossed the bag, landing it directly in front of her mother on the cooking island. "See mom. It's more than a treat. It's more than food. It's time well spent rewarding yourself by eating something thought-provoking and nurturing. You should try it."

Mattie started out on the mixing floor. All the surfaces lay flat and glinted steel or muted shades of white. Dust from the flour neither rose nor fell but seemed content to hang in the air, parting and then enveloping Mattie as she walked through. By the end of the day she looked like she had been operating a snow blower. Her eyelashes and the tiny hairs on the back of her hands were dusted with the white powder.

She began her job stationed in position 3. It entailed grabbing the flow tube and directing a 200-cup, perfectly measured, steady stream of flour, baking soda, sugar, and melted butter into the mixing machines. The mixing floor teetered on the edge of silence until she pressed the button on the left side of the flour hose. The pressurized cannon would unload the mixture with a loud pop and hiss. Always unprepared for the initial blast of pulverized dough, she was thrown back a few steps by the shots of forced flour. The avalanche would slam into the side of the rounded mixer and upchuck a good portion of the mash back into her face. This happened every time she moved to a new mixing drum. By the third day she had developed a rash that marched up both of her arms, over her neck, and into her hairline. Her cuticles had dried up and cracked back to the first knuckle. The state of her hands elicited gasps of disgust from her mother, which in turn, delighted Mattie.

Eventually, due to this allergy, she had to be moved to the line. She later learned the girls there called position 3 "getting frosted."

Mattie felt liberated after her first week. She was getting a new kind of weary look around her eyes, and she could feel the need for more comfortable shoes. She barely saw her mother at all.

Her evenings at home weren't as bad as she feared. Her father had stopped eating dinner at home a few years back, and her mom now seemed to have endless Junior League meetings. Really, it was about the same as it always had been. For the most part Mattie had been raised by the family's French-born nanny. She taught Mattie the language as well as how to speak her mind. They spent most afternoons crawling around the yard poking at beetles and watching squirrels hide nuts while Marie explained in English and French why everything deserved respect and a little bit of love. Unfortunately, Marie was gone in an instant when Mattie's mother overheard her thirteen-year-old daughter shyly telling Marie she had warm skin.

After Marie, everyone else was just hired help. Women who worked for her mother. Mattie felt sorry for them and spent hours trying to make it so they wouldn't have to work. She would serve them tea or ask them to help her brush a mat out of the dog's hair. They would smile at her and return to their unfinished chores. Mattie started to hate them almost as much as she did her mother.

In Mattie's preteen years, her parents took cooking classes and spent weekends throwing rollicking dinner parties for their friends. Her father labored for hours over pot roasts and briskets, concocting secret sauces by tossing in whatever lurked untouched in the spice cabinet. His meals were wild and unpredictable, sending his buddies into equal fits of disgust and delight.

The parties at the Friedlander's became legend as much for the main course as for the beautiful, intricate, delicate desserts that Mattie's mother created. Individual cupcakes topped with Eiffel Towers constructed with beams of chocolate. Fruit tarts displaying Monet's *Water Lilies*, painstakingly recreated with kiwis, pineapple, and guava bits. An hour later the drunken guests would haphazardly devour the treats while Mattie's mother ceremoniously accepted compliments and secretly admonished their lack of manners.

Working on the line was a completely different experience

than working on the mixing floor. The first difference: it was a very clean place. No flour dashing around or beaters thrashing about. And the ladies were not allowed to sit on stools. Jack claimed that sitting allowed the mostly 200-300-pound women to lean on the equipment, which in turn caused it to break. Third, she had coworkers. Mattie filled position 16, with Sara Lee on the right in 15 and Pat on her left in 17. They were the finishers.

Sara Lee had worked at the Midnight Delight factory for 12 years—all of them as a finisher. She was an uneducated woman but had always held a job. At Fireside, Sara Lee pulled the irregular facers off the belt. These were the misshapen and cracked baked pieces that could destroy the image of the manicured cookie should they make their way into a bag. Sara Lee's position was considered level 2 as it required her to make judgment calls as to whether a facer was 'heartfelt' enough to evoke fond memories in people.

Mattie's position had been open on and off for the last year. Fireside Farm was the last factory open in this part of Ohio. Campbell Soup, Fruit of the Loom, and Purina had all closed up and moved to Texas where the unions weren't as well entrenched. The labor force had either followed or left for Kentucky to make cigarettes. The unions eventually went too, leaving Fireside with few people to choose from during the busy cookie-making months. In addition, no one wanted position 16. The hot, semisweet chocolate burned your skin when it splashed up off the cookies. The acrid smell of the chocolate seared the inside of your nose.

None of those hazards concerned Mattie. She was too busy trying to keep up with Sara Lee.

Sara Lee was to Mattie as Ernest J. Keebler is to the rest of the elves. When the belt ran, her gaze never left the stage, and her eyes and hands moved with a grace and speed that her enormous frame could not match. She stood squarely on both feet and hummed while she pulled cracked and broken facers off and tossed them behind her into the refuse tub. Her hairnet rested right under her eyebrows, giving her a bit of a Kamikaze look. Sometimes she scared the shit out of Mattie.

Their tasks out on the line weren't all that complicated, and the simplicity of the work engulfed Mattie. The hum of the conveyor belt and the syncopation of the three women's hands created a lulling rhythm. After Sara Lee pulled the bad facers, Mattie squirted the chocolate on the good ones, and Pat merged them together with the dry facers. That's it. Mattie pulled the chocolate tube over and squirted as they rolled past her and towards Pat. The birth of the Midnight Delight.

There were a few trouble spots, and, more frequently than you might imagine, the cookies would get jammed up at the last juncture. Without Pat, disaster would ensue. When Johnny, the part-time substitute worker, filled in for Pat, cookies would get stuck together wrong, mangled and deformed, with facers gone solo and the occasional burping of one of their luxuriant nibblets onto the floor.

The first week on the line, Sara Lee didn't say a word to Mattie. Mattie would try to catch her eye and throw a smile at her, but Sara Lee would ignore her and continue humming. It wasn't until week two that Sara Lee called over to Mattie during lunch and asked her if she liked tapioca.

"Ah, doesn't everyone like tapioca?" Mattie replied.

"Then why ain't you eating yours?"

Mattie fingered the edge of her lunch bag and looked down at the tiny glass dessert dish. "It's, ah, crème brûlée."

"Well, don't sit there all day. Bring it over here if you ain't gonna eat it," Sara Lee declared with a floppy wave of her arm.

Mattie curled up what was left of her lunch in one hand and the dessert in the other. She sat down next to Sara Lee and gave her the dessert she had stolen from the bag her mother set aside every week for the housekeeper.

"That's almost too pretty to eat." She plunged her spoon through the crispy caramel-encrusted covering and into the creamy custard. She did away with it in three bites.

The first week in August, Pat came down with another bout of gout and Sara Lee and Mattie had to manage with Johnny. Mattie quietly despised Johnny. He interfered with the dance and was always bumping into her, causing her to spill searing hot chocolate on herself and sometimes even on Sara Lee. But Sara Lee, being the pro she was, organized the facers at the front end so after Mattie's earthshattering contribution, they flowed equally spaced to Johnny and then smoothly into the automated system. Like the leader of a marching band, Sara Lee lined up, held out, added, tossed, and paused facers.

When they broke for lunch, Mattie was determined to make sure Sara Lee knew her feelings. "You are an incredible worker. That is some amazing stuff you are doing back there. I have never seen anyone handle cookies like you do." Mattie immediately felt like an idiot for saying so.

Sara Lee looked around and leaned into her. "You don't want Jack on your ass, so you better stop watching what I'm doing," she whispered. "Just keep your hands on that squirter or you'll be back getting laid by Frosty."

Two hours later, back at the line, the debacle occurred. Sara Lee must have missed a few facers and the traffic jam began at the merge. Mattie behaved a bit like Lucy at the candy factory. She let go of the squirter and moved towards the cookies flying off the belt. But as soon as she did that she realized the facers were still coming and she leaped back to her position at the squirter. Sara Lee stood at her post as she had a hard time moving anywhere fast. Johnny just stepped back from the belt and stared. Cookies began to pile up and jump off the belt. It was chaos and Mattie panicked and yelled "Help!"

Jack came careening around the corner, hit the stop button and headed right past Mattie and towards Sara Lee. Sara Lee looked distraught as she rocked back and forth with her mouth gaping. The chaos and Sara Lee's momentary loss of composure made Mattie so nervous her hands started to shake.

Jack immediately turned to Sara Lee. "You stupid fat bitch," he said "What is wrong with you, yelling for help?" There were cookies everywhere and chocolate smeared on the belt where they had slid past on their way to the floor.

Sara Lee stood there.

"You spending all your fat time stuffing your face with our cookies. Is that what is going on here?"

Mattie was stunned and couldn't speak. Sara Lee stared at the floor as Jack crunched through the cookies and got up in her face.

"You're lucky you have a job here, you idiot." Spit flew from his mouth and landed on Sara Lee's hair. "Get this shit pile cleaned up. You got twenty minutes or you're out of here."

He kicked through the mound of cookies, spreading crumbs for a hundred feet and headed back to the office. Sara Lee turned around and started for the cleaning closet. Mattie held down a wave of nausea and took off after her.

"Sara Lee! Sara Lee!" Mattie whined. She caught up with her by the door of the supply closet. "You shouldn't let him talk to you like that, Sara Lee. I don't care if he is mad. That's disrespectful, not to mention he's creating a hostile work environment."

Sara Lee pulled back and laughed, "I ain't got no idea what you're talking about. So hush your mouth."

Mattie couldn't let it go. This was about working together for the common good. Mattie knew her constitutional rights, even if Sara Lee didn't. Mattie also knew about OSHA from the "Capitalism and the American Worker" course she had taken last fall. She made an A in that class, and it made her feel confident when she remembered the "excellent" and "good point" her professor had written on her final.

She thought about it some more that night while soaking

in the tub. She could hear her mother in the kitchen setting out cooling racks for éclairs. After the pastries cooled, her mother would tenderly engorge them with her special cream-cheese filling and dribble her hand-stirred chocolate sauce across the top. They would be waiting for the housekeeper to take home once she cleaned up all the pots and pans her mother had used to make them. Mattie could smell the warmed chocolate and thought how smooth and even it smelled when just barely melted.

The next afternoon, at the start of the lunch break, Mattie climbed the steps to the second-story office area. From here, Jack and his supervisors could see what was going on at all points in the cookie-making system. As she caught her breath, Mattie took off her hairnet and entered. She interrupted the semifinals in a game of Toe Jam between the supervisor of delivery and the head of packaging. The two semiobese men sat on opposite sides of the desk, each with one leg slung over the tabletop. The soles of their feet were held together by a rubber band while the great toes battled it out for supremacy. Mattie froze in the doorway. The men cheered on their favorite, not noticing Mattie until Jack looked up.

"What do you want, honey?" Jack eyed her up and down.

Mattie jumped and stuttered, "The incident yesterday at finishing . . . that was me who yelled for help, not S-a-ara Lee. I screwed it all up."

"So what?" Jack looked down at his shoe. "It's about what I'd expect from a fancy college girl like yourself." He finished unlacing his boot and cracked his toes back. The Toe Jammers stopped and all the men in the room turned to face her.

"You blamed the wrong person," Mattie said. "She didn't deserve to be yelled at like that. Not to mention, be called names and put down." Mattie felt stronger than ever.

Jack slowly slid his sock off, crossed his arms, and cocked a smile. "Well la-te-da, little missy. I don't give a shit what you think, so if you don't like it, march your ass right back down those stairs and head home."

She heard a few laughs from the men in the room and it made her stomach tighten. She stood her ground and held his gaze. "I don't know if you are familiar with the term *hostile work environment,* but it is a serious offense and there are laws in place to protect people like Sara Lee from people like you." The tone of her voice reminded Mattie of how her mother spoke to the gardener.

Jack jumped out of his chair and was at her in a flash. His boot skidded across the floor. He pointed his finger at the tip of her nose while the other supervisors nudged each other, smirked, and looked on.

"People like me, huh? What do you know about people like me, you high and mighty little twit? All parading in here for a little summer job and getting worked up into a lather when some fat black woman screws up and gets what's coming to her."

"Maybe you should be the one worried about what's coming." Mattie felt sick. She stared at him for a second or two with her arms stiff at her sides. Then she turned and stomped out.

Mattie stormed to the lunchroom and sat down next to Sara Lee with her back to the rest of the table. The other ladies took the cue and returned to their lunches. Mattie handed over an éclair from her lunch. Her ears felt hot and she wanted to cry. Sara Lee slowly munched through the dessert as Mattie delicately explained the protection from Jack to which Sara Lee was entitled by the U.S. government. She felt her strength come back as she recited her speech on employment law. Sara Lee listened intently and shook her head.

"I ain't interested in getting involved in all that crap. I ain't no leader or troublemaker. I'm just here to do my job and pay

my bills. I love you to death, honey, but don't bother me no
more with this foolishness."

"You're already involved, Sara Lee. I just had a talk with
Jack." Mattie dipped her chin and stared level at Sara Lee.

Mattie folded her t-shirts and placed them in a neat pile by
her suitcase. She had only her clothes to pack, as all her other
belongings had remained at school for the summer. Her hands
still wore the dark pockmarks where the heated chocolate had
splashed. She pressed down on them with her fingers, thinking
maybe she could smooth them away. The squeak of her
mother's matching Hermès belt and shoes announced her entry
into the room. She stopped behind Mattie, no doubt surveying
the packing progress. She patted Mattie on the shoulder before
she walked out. Mattie could smell the chocolate on her
mother's breath and it made bile rise in the back of her throat.

It was only six hours earlier that Sara Lee was called to the
office and fired. She came down the stairs with the same look
she wore when she was pacing the cookies. She didn't even
stop to get her thermos from the lunchroom. Mattie tripped,
running to catch her just outside the door.

Sara Lee shuffled across the parking lot, the dust drawing up
where her feet dragged across the ground. Mattie caught up to
her and had to shake her arm twice before Sara Lee looked.

Mattie blurted out the newest OSHA regulations and tried
to explain how they applied to Sara Lee's situation.

Sara Lee jumped at her, grabbed by the upper arm, and
spat, "You go on back to your college somewhere and be sure
and practice up on those laws. They were made for people
like you, not me." She threw down Mattie's arm and dug in
her purse. "Where's my goddamn bus coupon?" Mattie watched
her walk away across the parking lot. Sara Lee still had her
apron on. The strings dug a valley through the skin around
her waist and her knees brushed past each other as she trudged
towards the bus stop.

Mattie didn't return to the factory. After the bus hauled Sara Lee away, she got in her car and drove home with the top down. Her hair gnarled into knots it would take her days to untangle. She passed by her old high school and quietly rolled through the names of the friends with whom she had lost contact. She thought about her favorite college professors. She thought about Sara Lee and tried to imagine a future for her. She couldn't conjure up more than what she had just witnessed: the bus pulling back onto the road. She knew so little about the woman.

She turned onto her street and tried the same exercise for herself. She saw absolutely nothing. Less than nothing. Finally, she envisioned a bit of office work and perhaps more schooling. Oddly enough, this soothed her, and by the time she pulled into the driveway she had made up her mind not to return to the factory. She parked in the garage, closed the door behind her car, and walked into the kitchen. Her mother stood there, leaning against the counter staring into her cup of coffee. The oven creaked as it cooled.

WHY YOU HATE PINK

Deborah F. Lawrence

Your older sister bosses you around and makes fun of your best friend who lives across the street in the white house with pink shutters. Ginny calls your girlfriend Miss Wiggle-Bottom. It's true your friend has a slightly weird way of walking with her behind sticking out, but you are too polite to say anything about it.

Your mother has a song for everything. If you have a splinter in your finger, she might hum you right into the bathroom with a smooth song like "Begin the Beguine," right up onto the flesh-toned Formica counter, and continue humming as she opens the medicine cabinet and pulls out the splinter-removal kit that she keeps in a tin Band-Aid box. She uses a sewing needle, which she sterilizes with a burning match. As soon as you see that needle, you probably try to wiggle off the counter. But Mom has a song for that, too: "*It's now or never,*" sings Mom. "*Come hold me tight.*" You brace yourself against her and stare at the counter, which has a rubber-band pattern.

Pink is not your color. Mom dresses you in baby blue. Your sister gets the pink. Mom says that Ginny, who has dark brown hair and dark red lips, looks good in the rosy colors, and you look better in blue. Why? Because your hair is light brown? Because she wishes you were a boy? Is it something Mom learned in art school, where she developed so many opinions? The only pink clothes you get to wear are pajamas, underwear, and Ginny's hand-me-downs.

When Mom uses the needle she sings the bumblebee song:

> "*Bumble bee, Bumble bee, come from the farm,*
> *And sting little Betty right under the arm.*"

In a different situation this song is about tickling: Mom's finger is the bee; it swirls lazily around your head, then darts to your armpit when Mom gets to the word "sting." You start giggling and protecting your armpits when you hear the first words. But with the needle you don't know which part of yourself to protect. Is Mom kidding or serious?

She uses the needle to pierce the skin where the splinter is lodged throbbing in your finger, then she uses tweezers to pull it out. It's a horrible experience to be stabbed by Mom, but it's a relief to get the sliver of wood out. There's a song for that too, as you throw yourself off the counter and run out of the room:

> "*Trot little pony, London Town;*
> *Look out, little pony! Don't fall down.*"

You need to go to the bathroom, and your sister won't let you in. You could shove the door open, but why would you want to? Do you really want to see what Ginny is doing in there by herself? Is she working on a splinter? You wouldn't think of doing that for yourself.

You spend most of your time staying out of your sister's way so she won't hit you. If she wants to be alone in the bathroom, that is just fine. She loves to stare in the mirror, puckering her big red lips, brushing her glossy hair, practicing her ballet positions.

Once in a while, when you are alone with your sister and she isn't bossing you around, she brings up her two Burning Questions. You might be in the playhouse having a rare moment of domestic tranquillity, and she will ask, "Do you think we're adopted?"

Your understanding of the word is an alloy of orphanage scenes from Shirley Temple movies and fuzzy explanations of reproduction. You were there when Mom brought your new baby brother home from the hospital, before the family moved to California. He wasn't adopted. He came out of Mom's stomach. That's where you came from, too. "Do you think we're adopted and that's why Dad's so mean to us?" Ginny asks.

Her other question is: What does "mean" mean? It's a question that seems dumb to you. It's okay with you if one word sounds like another and means something else. You care about what things mean, but you don't care what "mean" means.

In the playhouse, Ginny is letting you cook. You concentrate on a mixture of pyracantha berries, rose petals, dirt, and water. You don't really think about it, you just answer her question: "Maybe *you're* adopted," you say. Almost instantly you realize it was a mistake.

116

"Shut up, Stupid," she says, giving you a big shove. "Get out of my playhouse."

You head for the back door to tell Mom. On the steps there's your cup of water and paintbrush. You get busy painting shapes on the hot concrete, watching the sun dry them almost as soon as they're painted. Your cowgirl hat makes a shadow on the step. The holes for the laces around the brim make points of light in the shadow.

Through the screen door you hear your baby brother gurgle, and the sound of Mom's rubber thongs flip-flopping on the kitchen linoleum. She's singing a song your brother likes:

> "*Someone's in the kitchen with Dinah,*
> *Someone's in the kitchen I know-oh-oh-oh,*
> *Someone's in the kitchen with Dinah, strumming on the old*
> *banjo.*"

When she gets to the part that goes "*Fee-fye-fiddly-eye-oh*," your brother cackles.

You know you're not adopted. You came out of Mom's stomach the way your brother did. You saw Mom get fat, then she came home with a tiny baby, and her stomach was flat again. Now it's fat again. Didn't Ginny see the same thing happen when Mom had you? Did your sister just forget?

Ginny runs up the steps to the back door and knocks over your cup of water with her foot. You shriek and watch the spill spread across your neat brushwork. The edges of the big water start to dry up.

There is no point in having a Burning Question, but if you did, it might be: Why is your sister so mean?

You lunge into the bathroom. Ginny is sitting on the toilet with her peach-colored pants up. She has Mom's splinter kit spread out on the counter, and she is poking her index finger with the needle. She looks up with solemn eyes. Is she crying?

"Let me in," you say, though you've already entered. "I have to go." You close the door behind you.

Your sister stays on the toilet. "I can do this and it doesn't hurt," she says. Her mouth goes back into a straight line.

You stand as far back against the door as you can. "Why are you doing that?"

"I can poke myself without crying," says Ginny. "Watch this."

She draws the needle back and slowly sticks it back into the tip of her finger.

"Ouch," you say for her. "Doesn't that hurt?"

"It hurts but it doesn't hurt," she says. You watch the needle come out and a drop of blood form. You hate to see blood. She puts her finger in her mouth and looks at you. Her eyes don't have tears but they are red.

"But why are you *doing* that?" you whisper.

"I'm practicing," she says. "I'm practicing not crying so when Dad's mean to me I won't cry."

You look at her and the tools on the counter. You know what she means about not wanting to cry in front of Dad.

"Why don't you tell Mom?" you ask.

"Mom doesn't care. She just hides when he yells."

"Mom's not hiding," you say. "She's busy." But it's true. Mom is never in the room when Dad gets mad. It's a good idea to get out of his way. If you have to face him when he's mad, you cry. It's impossible not to. But when Ginny faces Dad, she doesn't cry.

"You always act so brave with Dad," you tell your sister.

She smiles that straight line with her lips. "That's because I'm not a baby," she says.

A year later, your dad takes you shopping. Going to stores is your mother's job, but for Larry Hazen's birthday party you need a boy gift. Dad takes you to J.J. Newberry. You are excited to be looking at sporting equipment for the first time. Your Dad picks out a baseball and bat for Larry. Deep inside you know this is important: that you won't get to keep the ball and bat because they are boy's toys. You feel excluded from something big, and it feels terrible, like choking or drowning.

Your mom gives you light blue tissue paper. She lets you wrap up the ball and bat. You sniff the smoky place on the bat where words are burned into the wood. Your mom watches out of the corner of her eye. She is pregnant with your little sister. She sings "*Nobody knows the trouble I've seen, nobody knows my sorrow*" at the kitchen sink.

You wear a pale pink dress to Larry's birthday party. It is your older sister's hand-me-down and it's too big around the waist, made of chiffon with a stiff skirt pleated in hundreds of tiny folds that stick out too far and reach below your knees.

Four years later, your family moves out of the San Gabriel Valley because Dad wants to breathe better air. They buy the Alta Mar Motel. It's a whitewashed Spanish-style place on the beach with coral trim and a 7-Up machine. Your parents are busy every day renting units, cleaning units, fixing broken things in units, removing tar from carpeting. Your dad's in a better mood because he's his own boss and it's not at a drafting table. Your mother whistles while she works. You and Ginny and the little kids spend days on the beach. Everybody has a tan. Your skin turns the color of Band-Aids. Ginny is learning to surf. You are reading the Trixie Belden mysteries. You learn how to sneak into the soda machine with a key and liberally help yourself to strawberry soda.

One day, in a break from the routine, your dad leaves Mom to run things at the motel. He's driving you to the library. Usually Mom takes you, but today it's just you and Dad. You have one book to return: *Adopted Jane*, which you have read twice. It has a magenta cover.

You recognize the library but Dad drives past the parking lot. "Mom parks there," you say.

"Well, we're going here," says Dad. He parks on the street in front of one of those houses that somebody made into an office. He comes around to your side and takes your hand as you slide out of the car. "Leave your book," he says.

You realize this isn't a trip to the library.

"This is a doctor," says Dad. "Your Mom and I are worried about you. You might be sick."

You are the only people in the waiting room. The office has that horrible smell that doctor's offices have. You are too alarmed to say anything to your dad. There is a part of you that knows you are sick. You haven't been able to keep up with Ginny when you walk to the neighborhood market. She has to wait on almost every corner, yelling, "Hurry up, Stupid!"

The doctor is an old man with a few greasy hairs on his head. He sticks a needle in your finger and gets a drop of blood. He tells you to pee into a cup. Then he gives you a shot. It's the worst doctor visit you've ever had.

When you get home Ginny wants to know what happened. You tell her about all the needles. At the same time, Mom and Dad talk in the kitchen. Everything happens really fast, then really slow. You're in the car with Mom and Dad but the other kids have to stay home, with Ginny in charge. While Dad drives, Mom holds you on her lap in the front seat, which is unheard-of, especially for a ten-year-old. Mom doesn't say much, and she doesn't sing or even hum. You feel her arms holding you, and your mind stays blank with the unknown. There is everything wrong with this picture, but it is important that Mom is holding you. It's important that Dad doesn't even talk.

The Scripps Clinic is almost an hour from home, near San Diego. It's a beautiful rose-colored building with a tile roof, overlooking the beach in La Jolla. But you won't notice much about the beauty until a week later, when you are on your way out of the place. For five days you are mostly alone in a room, except when a doctor or nurse comes in. They teach you how to give yourself an insulin shot in your leg, and you do it every day. Three times a day you pee into a cup, and use a dropper to measure ten drops of urine and five drops of water into a test tube, then drop in a pill and watch the mixture turn color, then record the results on a chart. They give you a book called *Diabetic Manual* and a leaflet called "Mr. Hypo Is My Friend."

After a couple of days your dad comes to visit you. He brings you a copy of *Jack and Jill* magazine. He says you can leave the hospital, but he just means for a little while. You put on your clothes, and he takes you in his Porsche to a bookstore. He lets you pick out two new books for yourself: *The Borrowers* and *Honestly, Katie John!* It's the first time you've shopped for your own books. Usually Dad likes to bring home used books, like *Children of the Soil*, a strange, purple-bound book from the Soviet Union with cheap, yellowed pages and strange misspellings of English that you read and puzzle over. It's about a poor farm family.

You know that the special trip to the bookstore means Dad loves you. In the hospital you have time to read each book twice. One is about miniature people who live a complicated but happy, invisible life under the floorboards of a house. The other is about an eleven-year-old tomboy who speaks her mind and gets into trouble.

The days in the hospital seem to last forever. Outside the window there is blue sky and palm trees, and you can see La Jolla Cove, with people coming, swimming, and going. There's no one to talk to. There's no music and nothing to sing about. Once in a while a nurse comes in for a blood sample or trays arrive loaded with unpleasant food like soft-boiled eggs that you'll flush down the toilet. You sit on the bed in your pink, puff-sleeved pajamas, drawing in your sketchbook and reading, trying not to think about what the hospital people have been telling you: that your life will never be the same after this. You will always have to take insulin. You will never get to eat candy. And you will always have to be very, very careful about your feet.

You wonder why this has happened to you and not to your sister. You suspect that it has something to do with the amount of time you have spent at home studying the medical encyclopedia, fascinated by the pictures of children with polio, tuberculosis, and diabetes. You must have concentrated too hard and made yourself sick. Your sister, who hates to read, never wastes her time with books.

Finally, your mom comes with your sister for a visit. You stand with Mom and Ginny by the window and look out at the beautiful view of La Jolla Cove. "*Red sails in the sunset,*" sings your mom softly, even though it's a bright day. Your sister is silent, except to let you know that she had to return *Adopted Jane* to the library and pay the fine. You accept this solemnly as a demonstration of sisterly nurturance.

Right beside the window is a counter with some diabetes supplies on it: a vial of insulin, a syringe, alcohol swabs. Ginny is looking at them with interest. A nurse comes in with a big navel orange sitting on a tray alongside a little vial of clear liquid.

The nurse explains to your mom and your sister about injecting insulin. She tells them an orange is a good thing to practice on. She hands you the little vial that contains water instead of insulin. She explains what you're doing as you expertly stick the sharp needle into the little rubber stopper in the top of the bottle and draw out fifteen units of water. She points out that any member of the family can help the diabetic with her medication. You feel a flush of pride about your polished expertise in handling the equipment. As you pinch the flesh of the orange and quickly insert the needle like a dart, there's a sudden blur. Your sister Ginny has collapsed on the floor in a faint.

Five years later, you and Ginny have your own apartment at the Alta Mar: number 13, which is the hardest one to rent. It's a long narrow room without much light because it's built into the embankment between the beach and Pacific Avenue. The walls are painted an unfortunate shade of lavender because the old manager that Dad hired had the brilliant idea of turning number 13 into a bridal suite.

At opposite ends of the room, your beds are arranged as far apart as possible, and an Indian print bedspread separates you from your sister. Dad won't let you damage the walls with thumbtacks, but you have your art projects taped up on your side of the room, drawings of long-legged girls in Carnaby Street clothes. Your sister has the record player on her side, the stack of records leaning with her Jimi Hendrix album prominent.

A little bridge separates you from the house where the rest of the family lives. It's gotten too crowded in there now that there are five kids. Every morning, you cross over to the house in your pajamas, lift your syringe out of the pan where your mother has already sterilized it in boiling water, get your insulin out of the refrigerator, and draw out your dose. You carry it into your parents' bedroom and lie down on your mother's bed with your pants down. She comes in and shoots it in your butt. You just don't feel like doing it yourself. These few moments are your time of privacy with your mother. The little kids have to wait outside.

For the eighth-grade Valentine dance, you buy yourself a new outfit at Tot-to-Teen in downtown Oceanside: a pink, short-sleeved poorboy sweater, a pink hip-hugger skirt, and a wide white belt that matches the white go-go boots you got for Christmas, which zip up the back.

When you model the outfit for your mother you expect her not to like it because it's pink. But she doesn't come right out and say it. She smiles a tight smile with her lips together. Your littlest brother clowns around her ankles. She drags him with her to get closer so she can touch the shoulder of your new sweater. She says, "Hmm, wool. That should be hot on the dance floor." You can already feel sweat flow under your arms as she says it.

"Does it make me look fat?" you say, turning your well-fed self around for her as your brother tries to unzip your boots. You fend him off and he starts to whimper as you sidestep him.

"No," says Mom automatically. "It makes you look like you're . . . growing up," she tells you, as she stamps and sways to distract the baby from crying. "*Big boys*," she sings to him, "*don't cry-y-y, they don't cry. Big boys don't cry.*"

"Who says they don't cry?" you chime in, meanwhile wishing your mother would stick to music from her own age group instead of ripping off teen songs.

In most ways, having an apartment separate from the family is fine. You have your own bathroom, and a black-and-white TV, on which you watch the late afternoon teenage dance shows. Sometimes your sister watches too, but now Ginny is a senior and you are a freshman, so there isn't a lot of discussion. She leads a separate hippie life.

Besides having to breathe a lot of incense, the bad part about sharing the apartment is that Ginny lets her boyfriends in at night. You lie in your bed in the dark and listen while they have sex. It starts out quiet then it gets louder and louder, with your sister moaning and the guy grunting.

One night you're lying there, silently mouthing the words to "Eve of Destruction," trying not to listen to the animal sounds coming from your sister and whoever the current boyfriend is.

> "*And you tell me, over and over and over and over again,*
> *my friend,*
> *That you don't believe we're on the Eve of Destruction.*"

Someone knocks on the door. It's on your side of the room, but you pretend to be asleep.

Ginny passes your bed to get to the door. In the dark you can see she's totally naked. She pops the lock and opens the door a crack.

"Hey, man, what's happening," says a male voice. It's not your dad, who wouldn't bother to knock, anyway.

"Hey, man, I've got another cat in here," says your sister.

She goes back to bed, and pretty soon the moaning starts again.

The next day after school, you're alone in number 13, following the choreography of the teenage TV couples on the *Lloyd Thaxton Show*. You dance in front of the television, your thumbs cocked in the belt loops of your pink hip-hugger skirt. The skirt and the sweater, no longer new, both have permanent stains down the front from when you threw up on the gym floor at the eighth-grade dance last year.

As you shuffle to "Papa's Got a Brand New Bag," your sister bursts into the room. So she won't make fun of your dance moves, you quickly drop to a sitting position on the bed, sort of like James Brown. It's Ginny's bed. But your sister ignores this, tosses her shoulder bag and notebook on the floor. She's wearing an earth-colored granny gown and a magenta shawl.

"Hi! Watching the teenyboppers?" she says in an unusually friendly way. She sits down next to you in front of the TV.

"Not really," you say.

"Hey," she says. "It's cool." The way she says it, it means "That's okay."

You watch side by side for a minute. The James Brown song ends and Lloyd Thaxton appears in his flashy suit.

Ginny says, "Wow, that was a close one."

"What?" you say.

"Last night, man. When Bobby Brinegar came to the door and I already had Carl in here."

You look at her out of the corner of your eye, still facing the TV. Wait a few beats.

"What if Dad found out?" you say.

Ginny stands up. "You better not tell him," she says.

"I'm not," you say. "I won't." But you wish you could. You can't tell Mom, she's too busy. You are alone with the information.

"If Dad found out, though—" you say.

"Fuck him," says Ginny, and the word scorches your ears. "He has no right to call me a tramp and lay his trip on me when he is just as bad." She looks at you squarely. "You know he's fooling around on Mom, don't you?"

No, you don't. Your dad is too busy. Your mom is too much of a saint. It would be too sad. "No way," you say.

"For real," says your sister. "Why do you think he can't stop talking about that Helen Mudd lady?"

Dad is always talking about something at the dinner table, the Kennedys, whatever. You just have to act like you're listening. It's true he's been talking about Helen Mudd a lot. He calls her "a great gal." He met her at the Democratic Club. "So? That doesn't prove anything," you say. But a slow, sickening feeling creeps into your throat.

"Well, Mom told me he's having an affair with her." Ginny pauses while the trashy words resonate. "And the next time he calls me a slut I'm going to throw *that* in his face," says Ginny.

"You're crazy," you say. But you feel nauseated.

"No, I'm not," says Ginny. Her eyes are wide, her lips are red and grimacing through her flaking white lipstick. "Our dad's a jerk, Betty. Just in case you hadn't noticed."

Your mind races around between pictures of your dad and your mom, separated by a picture of a lady you've never even seen. The word "affair" conjures up flat cartoony scenes from *Love, American Style.* Not your dad with his push broom. Not your mom with your littlest brother. Your poor mom. It's too much to think about. You feel tears leaking out of your eyes. You look down at your stained pink sweater. Are you going to throw up?

Your sister's mood changes. She says, "Hey, maybe I shouldn't have told you that. You're so young and innocent." She stands up and crosses the room. You watch her movements without comprehending them. They are filtered through a curtain of shock. She picks up her purse off the floor. She fumbles in it and pulls out a Band-Aid box.

"You want a toke?" she says. She shakes the box and it rattles. "It's Afghani," she says. "You might really like it."

She goes back and locks the door. She opens the Band-Aid box and pulls out matches. She lights a stick of incense that's already wedged into one of the perforations on top of the TV. Then she dumps out the rest of the box's contents on the bed: a folded square of foil, a sewing needle, and a lump of brown stuff that you suppose must be marijuana.

"Check this out," she says. She rolls the foil into a little hollow tube. She squeezes one end closed and uses the needle to poke some holes in the foil. This she hands to you. "Hold it still," she says, as she pinches a chip of brown stuff off the lump. She holds it under your nose. "Smell," she orders. "Guaranteed to put you out of your misery."

You can hardly believe what is happening. You dangle between the brand-new, unimaginable possibility that your father is more of a creep than you ever realized, and the miracle of sharing intimate space with your sister without being criticized or bullied. She seems to be inviting you into her world. Obviously, it's a dangerous place, but you are fifteen years old. You have to grow up sometime.

You sniff. It's a strong dirt scent. The smell distracts your brain from pictures of your mother as you've seen her recently, crying on the back steps for no reason.

The setting sun comes in the window and turns the lavender walls of number 13 a deep, violent rose.

A Bull's Eye

Elizabeth McCarthy

Granny pulled her car into the narrow driveway, carefully avoiding a jumble of empty packing boxes stacked on the concrete. Splashes of brown covered her wrinkled hands. Wisps of white hair curled around her brow. Her eyes, the color of faded denim, guarded a small face crossed by lines. She stared at the white, two-story house.

E.T. bounced down the back stairs two at a time. A surge of pride filled her heart as she climbed carefully out of the car. E.T. planted a kiss on her cheek.

Granny held her twelve-year-old grandson at arms' length for a better look. E.T. had big feet and hands, and his blond hair never stayed combed. He stood half a head taller than

Granny, and his deep blue eyes sparkled with what she called youthful exuberance.

The boy had become used to his name although Granny had never liked the initials, E.T. He'd been called Alien and Mars Bar and once, in the third grade, by his archenemy Jack, Edible Turnip. He really was Elwood Timothy Martin Junior, but to avoid Junior his father had called him E.T., and the name had stuck.

"A good day for a party in our new house, yeah, Granny?" He looked at the big building. Granny nodded and clutched her coat against a brisk wind and moved toward the steps.

At the top of the stairs, E.T. raised his hand and said, "Granny, wait, look at this." The front hedge danced an advance-and-retreat kind of step across the side yard. "Did you see that? The hedge stretches like a rubber band then flies back out of sight. Magic, yeah?" Granny shivered and glanced at the red lip of a winter sun hovering above the mountains.

"That's right, E.T., almost alive . . . Might be snow tonight, child . . . It's cold."

They left their shoes in the mudroom and entered the kitchen where Elwood stood stirring gravy. Sweat beaded his forehead and dampened tufts of gray that framed his face. Laugh lines at the corners of his eyes had deepened to furrows.

"Hi, Mom." Elwood spoke without lifting his gaze from the brown liquid. He leaned a cheek toward her for a kiss as he scraped the edges of the pan. "How's my best girl?"

"Real fine. The smell of that beef makes me hungry." Granny lifted the towel covering a standing rib roast. "Looks good enough to eat. You've become a good homemaker, Elwood."

"Couldn't have done it without you and Jess and April." He turned the burner to low. Granny dipped a teaspoon into the gravy for a taste and nodded that he'd gotten it right.

Years had passed since all the brothers and sisters had been together, yet Granny could still see the long table, the glowing candles, and rows of silverware on each side. She could see a Tom turkey or a roast and smell fresh bread. But best of all, she could hear the laughter of her children and their friends. Where had the laughter gone, she wondered.

Still fondling the memory, Granny went to the closet to hang her coat.

As she finished, Jess and Willis arrived carrying presents and a bottle of wine. Jess had light brown hair and eyes that matched. She unzipped lizard-skin ankle boots and set them beside Elwood's Nikes. Granny nodded at Jess and waited her turn to say hello. As Willis stepped out of his black suede loafers, he pointed to a rifle standing in the corner of the foyer.

"You expecting trouble, Elwood?"

Elwood grinned at his brother-in-law. "No, that's E.T.'s BB gun, got it for him last summer."

E.T. grabbed the gun and sighted it at the neighbor's kitchen window where three people worked at an island counter.

Elwood's face fell. "Damn it, boy! You know better than to point a gun at people."

"Sorry, Dad." E.T. handed the BB gun to Granny. Then he gave Jess a hug and put the packages in the dining room.

"Make yourselves at home," Elwood said and headed to the roast of beef on the kitchen counter. Granny set the gun in the corner and hugged Jess and Willis. Jess had made a special effort to come to her nephew's party that day. Being a second-year ministerial student meant she was busy Sundays, and Willis, when he wasn't with her, occupied himself with what he called entrepreneurial adventures.

Elwood sharpened the carving knife with the flare of a Samurai and began to cut. Thin pink slices curled away from the roast. "Perfect!" he yelled. Jess dished up Brussels sprouts and cauliflower. Granny whisked potatoes and piled them into a serving dish with a dollop of butter.

Earlier, E.T. had put name cards at each place. He had

even arranged two white candles as a centerpiece. Persimmon-colored coals winked in the fireplace nearby. Elwood asked E.T. to light the candles and announced that dinner was ready.

At that moment, April, wearing a full-length mink coat and carrying a foil-wrapped package, blew in through the front door. Her corn-colored hair covered her face. While she removed her boots, she chattered nonstop about the increased traffic on the hill. April was Granny's youngest child. After college she started her own telecom business. Sometimes she hired E.T. to file and dust. She had barely gotten to her chair when the doorbell rang again.

Granny answered it. E.T.'s friend swaggered in, wearing oversized jeans and a scrubbed Ivory look. His hair glistened with gel. He said hello to Granny, dropped his coat on the floor by his shoes and marched over to shake hands with Elwood. E.T. followed.

"This is John. He's in my class."

John smiled shyly.

Elwood motioned for everyone to sit down. What came to mind as Granny watched her middle-aged son was the chubby sixth grader he had been, the boy with mischief in his eyes; then the turbulent adolescence, the troubled marriage, the hideous divorce, and now a plateau.

The group clasped hands and bowed heads as Jess said the blessing in her Sunday voice. She blessed E.T. and John and all family members, finally getting to the food. "Amens" popped up like grace notes from around the table when the prayer ended.

Willis poured wine for those with wineglasses, and Elwood got Frescas for the boys and himself.

"Seahawks can't seem to pull off a win for anything. Lost again today. What do you think of 'em, Elwood?"

"Haven't been watching. E.T. and work fill my days. The new manager not doing well?"

"My Daddy says he's given up on 'em," said John. "We're waiting for Mariner games . . . Already got season tickets."

"Dad, can we get season tickets, please?" E.T. stabbed the air with his fork.

"We'll see. Maybe a five- or eight-game package, if work keeps up."

"Promise?"

Elwood hesitated before answering and when he did, he looked directly into his son's eyes. "Promise." Granny was glad to see Elwood hesitate because it meant that he remembered what she had tried to impress on the children, that a man's word is his bond.

While Willis refreshed April's wineglass, he asked, "April, you hear the one about the presidential candidate politicking at the nursing home?"

"Nope, and I hope it's not one about the present administration. You might push me too far, Willis." April and Willis always bantered back and forth, if not about politics then about business.

Willis grinned like he had a fish on the line and set the bottle down. "A candidate entered a nursing home hoping to win some votes. Near the door sat a little old lady in a rocking chair. 'Do you know who I am?' he asked in a honeycomb voice. The old lady looked him over. 'Can't say as I do, but down there is a nurse, she can tell you.'"

The guests all laughed except April. Granny muffled hers in a napkin. She vowed never to be the little old lady near the door. Not her. She'd keep her wits clear and her mind active right up to the end.

"You're making fun of my candidate, Willis. I know it," said April. She sipped her wine.

"Hey, didn't use a single name, but you know he can't say who he is till the polls or his advisors tell him, got to admit that," said Willis.

Elwood carried the cake in from the kitchen to the accompaniment of the birthday song. On top, a snowboarding figure stood ready to shoot down a trail between green candy trees on slopes of white frosting. Candlelight reflected on Elwood's moist face as he set the cake in front of E.T., who blushed and hung his head. John covered his face and whether he stifled a sneeze or laughter, it was hard to tell. E.T. extinguished the flames with a giant blow, leaving twelve corkscrews of smoke twisting in the air.

While Jess served ice cream and cake, E.T. opened presents. The first was a computer game Jess knew he wanted. The card showed a girl's face blowing a kiss. Granny's card came next, mushy, but the money it contained made up for that. While the three siblings chatted, Willis stepped into the hallway and returned carrying the BB gun. He sighted it at an embossed chrysanthemum on the far wall.

At the other end of the table, Elwood held up the card with the girl blowing a kiss. "Hit this, Willis!" Willis was from Texas where a man's rifle is sacred and young boys learn early to shoot.

Willis squinted and took a bead on the card.

"Get something, Elwood," shrieked Granny, "you're going to shoot pellets into the wall!"

"Wait, Willis." Elwood raised his hand and left the room. A few minutes later he returned with two quarter sheets of plasterboard, which he propped, one on top of the other, on a chair. "Now," he said as he pinned the card to the board. The ladies fanned their chairs away from the table. John's eyes grew as big as dollars and E.T. inched forward to the edge of his chair.

Willis put on his black felt hat. He stood tall, took a breath and squeezed off a shot. BANG! The BB cut a perfect hole just above the nose. John and E.T. ran over to see. "Wow! That's awesome." Willis shot a few more times, then Elwood, and finally E.T. Not one of them hit the nose. Jess, April, and Granny followed the action like Wimbledon spectators.

"You're a natural," Granny said as E.T. hit the finger holding the kiss. "I used to shoot snakes in the lake with my Uncle Clyde's .22 when I was your age."

"Tell the truth, Granny. Did you ever hit any?"

"I certainly did! I'd plug 'em when they came up for air. They have to breathe, you know."

John wanted to shoot, but Elwood said no because he hadn't been trained.

"Over here, E.T." April held up the foil-wrapped box. He ripped away the wrapping and held up what appeared to be a white athletic shoe.

"Cool, soap shoes," he shouted. E.T. explained that soap shoes have a two-inch steel arch made to slide along ledges and railings like a skateboard. He stumbled across his own foot getting over to hug April.

When the doorbell rang, E.T. answered it. Two policemen in full uniform stood on the porch. Elwood had seen the blue and white cruiser pull up in front of the window and in no time was on his feet.

"Hello, young man, your father in?" the taller one asked.

"Yes, sir." E.T.'s expression was sober as he turned to his father.

"I'm Elwood Martin, officer." He ran his fingers through his mop of ash-colored hair as he approached. "Come in. This is my family." He led them to the table.

Young enough to be my grandsons, Granny thought. The shorter one wore a uniform that fit like Spandex. His close-set eyes darted around the room. The taller officer, Greg, smiled a lot, especially when he shook E.T.'s hand.

"Mr. Martin," Greg said, "we're responding to a report of gunfire coming from this address."

"Just an air rifle. We're having a birthday party for my son, E.T." Elwood pulled up two chairs. "Sit down, officers, have some cake and ice cream. Coffee's hot, warm you up." Granny went to the kitchen for plates and coffee. She left the door open. The rifle leaned against the back of the sofa that separated the dining room from the living room.

134

"This the piece, Mr. Martin? The report says two adults and a minor were involved." Officer Ellis inspected the gun and glanced at the plasterboard. "The target?"

Elwood said yes and glanced at the neighbor's house. Three figures stood backlit against the kitchen window. Granny brought in plates and coffee.

"Cake's real good," she said.

"No thanks, Mrs. Martin, we're on duty."

"Even a small piece?" Officer Ellis shook his head. Officer Greg talked about how pellets ricochet and put out people's eyes, emphasizing that an air rifle is a dangerous firearm. When the officers finished, they shook hands and said they'd enjoyed meeting the family.

"Remember, son, happy birthdays are safe birthdays." Officer Greg pulled the door shut behind him.

The minute the cruiser rolled out of sight a cacophony of voices erupted. Back at the table, Elwood slumped down in a chair and asked E.T. to bring in Frescas.

"Your neighbors suck," Willis said. He opened the soda with one hand.

"In the morning," Jess said pointing a finger at Elwood, "you go to Sears and buy drapes."

"The neighbors should have called you before the police. Does that go on your record?" April's face was serious.

"Oh, I'm sure there's a record. There's always a record." Elwood let out a sigh. His elbow rested on the table as he propped his head on his hand.

The sound of a gun being cocked reached all ears at the same time. Granny rose to a standing position holding a small, pearl-handled revolver, one hand cradled in the other. She sighted it at the target and squeezed.

KABOOM! The nose disappeared.

Granny lowered the gun. Elwood leaped up to flip off the light switch. Dandelion-puffs of light appeared mid-table in the sudden darkness. "Mom, what are you doing? You'll have us all in jail."

"That's for nosy neighbors." A silhouette thrown on the wall by the fireplace gave Granny huge proportions. For a moment her head brushed the ceiling, then the illusion vanished as quickly as it had appeared. She slid the gun into her purse and closed it.

"Why did you get a gun, Mom?" asked Jess.

"Yeah, Mom, tell us . . ." April appeared to be about one degree off full-blown laughter.

"I bought it when the government threatened to take away my right to own a gun, and it cost me a bundle to take lessons . . . I go to the range every other week to keep up my skill."

"Take me next time, Granny, please, please," wheedled E.T.

"Me, too, Mrs. Martin. I want to shoot like that." John had finally gotten a word into the conversation.

John and E.T. drifted off to the computer and, for a while, advice buzzed around Elwood like flies at a picnic.

The aunts and Granny tidied up and talked about their duties for the upcoming week. Elwood and Willis smoked cigars in the dining room. They drew diagrams to show how the new house could be divided into rental units. When drawings covered the entire plasterboard, Willis put down his pencil and said that he and Jess should go home.

With goodbyes chiming in the air, E.T. and Elwood walked Granny to her car. The wind had disappeared leaving only clear, bitter cold in its wake.

"Would you look at all those stars . . . A freeway for space ships." E.T. pointed to a brightness in the middle of the sky. The three stood there with their arms around each other gazing at the heavens until Granny's shivering cut short their wonder.

"Gosh, Granny, I never knew you could shoot like that," E.T. said.

"She's still got it, E.T.," said Elwood. Then, turning to Granny, he said, "Thanks for coming, Mom."

"Give me a hug, E.T.," Granny opened her arms. "From one shooter to another," she whispered in his ear, "guns aren't toys. If anything happened to you or your friends, my heart would break. Promise me you'll follow the rules, always." He drew back. His face reflected the earnestness of what he was about to say.

"Promise, Granny, always."

THE HIVE

Michelle Goodman

"With these ashes, the Evergreen Point campfire burns not just once a week, but all summer long, as each campfire is linked to the one before it and the one that will follow it, just as each of you is linked in sisterhood to the camper to your left and the camper to your right, throughout the summer, and for that matter, throughout the fall, winter, and spring, until we meet again next June . . ."

The camp director delivered the same speech every Friday night. Danielle knew Gert's sermon was supposed to evoke strong feelings of fondness for her fellow campers—and for Evergreen Point Sleepaway Camp for Girls. But it wasn't working.

"Look hard into these flames. These flames represent

friendship and sisterhood and love," continued Gert. She stabbed at the purpling sky with her shovel for emphasis.

A snickering erupted behind Danielle. The Fab Five. Or as Danielle liked to think of them, the Hive. The self-anointed Five knew each other either from school or temple. They had thick Long Island accents and a limitless supply of stiletto insults.

What had she done this time? Danielle nervously twirled a clump of her orange corkscrew bangs around a freckled finger. Her mother had insisted on a sensible summer trim. Danielle thought the cut made her look like Raggedy Ann with braces.

Maybe they were laughing at her frizzy mop of hair. Or the way she'd splayed her windbreaker next to her on the damp log to save a seat for Fran. The Five considered any transgression—no matter how insignificant—fair game. Wake up with a pimple on your forehead, and they branded you Cyclops for the rest of the day. Trip over your shoelace, and they immediately labeled you Mentally Retarded. Athletic faux pas were the worst offense. Blow the softball game for the team, and you became Whatta Douchebag! for the next week. Ratting out The Five to a counselor wasn't an option. Do so, and you'd hear Snitch whispered at your back every three minutes.

Danielle scratched at the mosquito-bite anklets forming along the flesh exposed by her high-water jeans. While camp shopping, Danielle's mother had given her the choice between French jeans and the training bras she wanted. She regretted not choosing the designer jeans. Harnessing her washboard breasts had done little to endear Danielle to her bunkmates. It hadn't changed the fact that her camp uniforms, the olive-green polo shirts with the pine-tree insignia over the left boob, were faded and frayed at the hems—hand-me-downs from the same cousin who donated the jeans. Nor did wearing a bra make up for her hair being too short to braid and too wiry to tame with barrettes. Or her ears not being pierced yet. Not until your bat mitzvah, her father had mandated. That was still a year away.

Danielle sucked in her breath. Where on earth was Fran?

Danielle wasn't sure she would make it through the final fifteen minutes of the campfire. She wished Gert would stop waving that shovel around and start digging already. She didn't exhale until Gert positioned herself at the base of the 124-year-old pine. Once there, Gert repeatedly plunged the shovel into the soft brown earth, tossing each heap over her shoulder. The spray of dirt flying from the rusty shovel briefly eclipsed Gert's head. A fair amount of the matter landed on the tennis visor she wore. Though old enough to be Danielle's grandmother, Gert quickly retrieved from the ground the tinderbox containing the last campfire's remains. Danielle couldn't help but marvel at the aging woman's strength and stamina.

The campfire drawing to a close promised only a temporary reprieve from the Fab Five. Unfortunately, the Five were in Danielle's bunk. Her only other bunkmates were Stacie and Steffie Simon, the twins from Connecticut. The twins hadn't been welcomed into the Hive, but they'd earned immunity from the Hive's sharp tongues by pretending Danielle didn't exist.

The entire bunk was entering the seventh grade that fall. But the Five seemed older. During rest period, while Danielle pored over comic books and crossword puzzles, the Five painted their toenails and scoured fashion magazines for tips on tongue kissing. These were girls who wore berry-flavored lip gloss and gold charm necklaces. They had pierced ears and tall, wavy tresses. Their budding breasts stood at attention beneath their crisp, immaculate camp polos. Anastasia Meyer's string bikini top revealed an abundance of cleavage. Nan Finkel shaved her legs and armpits daily. Wendy Rosenthal had once touched a boy's thing. Tamara Grant already knew how to drive a car.

The Five changed ringleaders every few days, so Danielle never knew whose path to steer clear of. This week it was Shannon Levine, who for three days straight had beaten the tennis instructor, rumored to once have been a pro. Shannon was forever changing her hairstyle. Yesterday she sported the

Princess Leia look. The day before, tight French braids. Today it was a loose bun with tendrils gently dusting either shoulder.

Each day at Evergreen Point Sleepaway Camp for Girls was a minefield of hand-eye-coordination activities—more fodder for the jeering Five. Tennis. Softball. Kickball. Volleyball. Badminton. Touch football. Archery. Ping-pong. Jacks. It was endless. To the exasperation of her counselors and the delight of her hypercompetitive bunkmates, Danielle was terrible at almost every sport.

Swimming was the activity Danielle dreaded most—both for the physical peril and the vast amounts of ridicule it invited. Her arms and legs would pucker with goose bumps as they flailed about the chilly lake water, and her hands and feet would go numb. She halfway expected the slimy tufts of seaweed that lapped at her ankles to drag her to the lake bottom. She held onto the spongy red kickboard for dear life and tried to keep the water from entering her lungs. Despite all Danielle's spluttering and botched attempts at bubble blowing, she could still hear the taunts of her bunkmates:

"Look at the retard. It'll take her all summer to pass the crawl-stroke test."

"Maybe she should be wearing floaties like the seven-year-olds."

"Can you actually drown in three feet of water? Because I think Danielle's doing it."

Danielle began making up excuses why she couldn't volley or bat or do the doggie paddle. She had a stomachache. A twisted ankle. A hangnail. Dandruff. Sometimes the sports counselors bought it and let her wander off and do as she pleased. More often than not, they wouldn't budge, and Danielle would have to grab a racket or kickboard and suck it up.

Today Danielle had faked a sprained ankle. Now, scratching madly at her foot, she thought it did in fact look a little swollen.

Danielle watched the stars that had begun to take their places in the night sky, above the evergreens. The Hive buzzed louder at her back, threatening to drown out the popping and hissing of the fire's pumpkin-colored embers. Before Danielle could determine what she had done to warrant their derision, she saw what they were laughing at. It was Lila, their bunk counselor. At last, the ceremony was winding down. But Lila was just arriving. She wobbled atop the soft dirt path in four-inch-high red suede clogs. With a golf ball-sized hickey on her neck.

Lila managed to teeter to the semicircle of rotting logs positioned around the campfire. She wedged herself between two counselors in the back row. Her boyfriend, Pete, the archery counselor, emerged slowly from behind the pines lining the dirt path. Gert paid no mind to the disturbance. She was too busy leading the camp in the Evergreen Point alma mater, which was actually "You've Got a Friend," but with different words.

Gert waved her shovel back and forth as though conducting a symphony. Danielle could pick out the voices of Tamara Grant and Shannon Levine harmonizing from the row behind her. She imagined them huddled together for warmth. Mouthing the words, Danielle shifted her bony rump against the clammy log bench. She picked up her windbreaker from the bench and draped it around her shoulders. Fran clearly wasn't coming to the campfire. She was always getting out of attending things.

Despite what her weekly letters told her parents and friends back in New Jersey, Danielle couldn't wait until camp was over. Only four more weeks to go. At least she had the art shack. There, she felt safe, peaceful even. It was her one refuge.

The morning after the campfire, Danielle made a beeline for the art shack. She and Fran had planned to get an early start making an origami wildlife preserve. Danielle was in such a hurry to meet Fran she didn't stop at the bunk after breakfast to floss.

The art shack was situated on a hill with an overgrown lawn, at the far eastern corner of the camp property, just ten or twenty yards from the lake. Its creaky front porch offered a view of the entire camp: The mess hall where the campers downed dinners of charred burgers, soggy corn-on-the-cob, and vanilla/chocolate/strawberry ice-cream bars. The rec hall where they watched movies on rainy afternoons, and the boathouse storing the kayaks and canoes the counselors and older campers used. To the west of the mess hall lay the bunks, swimming docks, and campfire circle. In the distance, they were as small as matchbooks.

Danielle could easily spend half an hour gazing out the back windows of the art shack onto the calm water. Makeshift wind chimes of sardine cans and eating utensils tinkled at the back door. It was beautiful, this lake ringed by evergreens that seemed to stretch to the clouds. It was nothing like home, in so many ways. Home was a land of cul de sacs and sidewalks and supermarkets and gas stations. There were book reports, extra-credit projects, and chores to do. Test grades and cleaned rooms for her parents to inspect. Friends to walk home from school with, girls she had played with since first grade.

There were only two art periods a week at camp—this in contrast with the twenty-odd periods devoted to one humiliating sport or another. Whenever Danielle could escape an activity or a meal, she went to the art shack. Craig, the camp's only counselor with both a ponytail and a beard, ran the shack. There, Danielle could make lanyard necklaces, copper enamel pendants, god's eyes, collages, dioramas, and Popsicle-stick architecture. She could use the loom to weave trapezoid-shaped potholders and the kick wheel to throw asymmetrical bowls. She could develop her own photos in the darkroom downstairs. She could even reverse the black and white in the pictures, so people's faces looked dark and their hair and clothes light.

No matter what she made, Craig would examine it from every possible angle, look intently at her with red-rimmed eyes, and say it was good. Danielle worshipped Craig.

Last week Danielle made a macramé choker with a bead in the middle. Craig said it was a most beautiful creation and asked if she wanted to donate it to the shack's Wall of Inspiration. Her ribcage heaving, Danielle gazed from one corner of the shack to another. She wanted to breathe the room in, like freshly cut flowers from her mother's garden. The late afternoon sun filtered into the room in chunky beams, each one suspending millions of dancing dust particles. Rainbows formed by crystals hanging in the windows crept along whitewashed walls like giant gemstone spiders. Joni Mitchell's velvety voice beckoned from the record player, and the burgundy beaded curtain hanging in the doorway shimmied in the breeze. Danielle felt woozy with delight.

She didn't want to disappoint Craig, but she wanted to savor that wondrous feeling. She put her fingers to the bead at her neck, then ran a tentative hand over the red spirals on her head. She told Craig she wanted to wear her new necklace for a day or two.

The next afternoon at tennis, Nan Finkel asked nicely where Danielle had gotten her choker.

"You made that? It's so good!" Nan offered.

The sun reflecting off the hot concrete felt good on Danielle's face. She angled her head and shut her eyes for a few seconds, allowing herself to bask in her bunkmate's momentary admiration. The sun glowed orange and red behind her eyelids.

"Hey, you guys, look what Danielle made!" Nan waved the rest of the Hive over.

The girls cooed sweetly, as though they were all the best of friends. They wanted to try it on. Danielle put a protective hand to her throat and explained the only way to remove the choker was to cut it off. They wanted her to show them how to make one. Danielle refused. She wanted to be good at something no one else could do.

"Fine, then we'll make them ourselves!" Nan Finkel snapped. When the Five returned from art period later that week with five identical macramé chokers, Danielle threw her own choker away.

Craig was rarely at the art shack this early. But Fran always was. Fran was a year older than Danielle. She was from a Jersey town fifteen minutes up the parkway from Danielle. She had braces, a stocky frame, and a protruding belly that she hid under blousy Indian-print shirts and thick denim overalls. She never wore the camp shirt.

Fran referred to the art shack as the Oasis. Like Danielle, she hated her bunkmates. Fran called her bunkmates the E Girls. They were girls whose names ended in the "ee" sound: Jenny, Shari, Carrie, Amy, Jessie, Missy. Fran's only other bunkmate, Barb, talked about masturbation incessantly.

The E Girls weren't into anything cool like reading mysteries or making up comic strips. They were too busy applying makeup and practicing their tennis serves. Fran said they probably would all become cheerleaders, sorority sisters, and ultimately, suburban housewives. Danielle chuckled in agreement without entirely understanding what Fran meant.

No matter what time of day Danielle hit the art shack, Fran was there with the same greeting: "What's shaking, Red?" After flashing her orthodontia at Danielle, Fran would keep her nose in her sketchbook. Periodically she'd raise her head, tuck her greasy black hair behind an ear, and offer commentary on a camper she didn't like. Sometimes she'd even do it during a regularly scheduled art period, when her target was there.

Fifth period Tuesdays and second period Thursdays were the official art periods for Danielle's bunk. Cupping her hand around Danielle's ear, Fran whispered that both Simon twins had nose jobs. Bad ones. She put Danielle in stitches with her pantomimed hair primping every time Shannon Levine strutted by. And she once passed Danielle a note that read, "Why does everyone have painted nails? Don't they know this isn't prom night?"

Fran used words Danielle wasn't allowed to use at home. She even used the *c*-word. When she was done editorializing, Fran would hold up whatever she had been drawing. Usually it was a comic strip character, like Dennis the Menace or Prince Valiant. They were flawless replicas of the ones you'd see in the Sunday morning newspaper. Danielle thought Fran was brilliant.

Sometimes big chunks of text would crowd Fran's comic strip characters on the pages of her sketchbook. Fran said they were poems about things that had happened to her lately, things that went on at home.

"Can I read one?" Danielle had asked once.

"Nah, they're too personal," Fran said. "If I caught anyone reading them behind my back, I'd kill them."

Danielle secretly hoped that before the summer ended she would see Fran in word-to-word combat with one of the dreaded Five. She knew her parents wouldn't approve of her befriending a girl with Fran's mouth. She found Fran pretty intimidating herself, but she admired Fran's brazenness. Fran's companionship was something of a dangerous pleasure, like Danielle rubbing herself between her thighs after school and praying her little sister wouldn't walk in.

Earlier in the week, Danielle was contemplating what Fran had said about killing anyone who read her poems, when Fran removed a ring from her pinky.

"Here. Keep it. My mother sends me a gift, like, every three days. I tried to tell her to stop, but it doesn't work."

Danielle slipped the silver ring on her middle finger. She thought it was weird-looking but pretended to admire it. It was shaped like a bear claw and had a piece of turquoise in the middle. Fran said her mom bought it at an Indian reservation out west. The bear claw symbolized good luck.

The sun was out, but the day wasn't getting any warmer. Fran was fifteen minutes late. Anxious, Danielle sat up straight, her midsection pressed hard against the worktable. She turned the bear-claw ring and picked at her cuticles. She rarely ran into Fran outside the art shack, not even at meals in the mess hall. It had been Fran's idea that Danielle save her a seat at last night's campfire. Fran had also suggested they meet in the shack this morning. Danielle wondered if Fran would show today.

Danielle selected a shiny purple paper square and began making the folds. A few moments later, Craig came up from the darkroom, smelling like smoke and breath mints. Danielle asked Craig why no one at camp cared that Fran did whatever she wanted. Danielle didn't hide her envy. Craig hinted that Fran's father had made some special deal with Gert. Something about not making Fran do anything she didn't want to because she'd had a tough year. Danielle wondered why. Had she gotten into trouble at school? Were her parents getting a divorce? Had she been diagnosed with some awful disease? Before Danielle could ask, Craig turned the volume on the stereo to 8.

Danielle surveyed her creations: a paper elephant, a giraffe, and two orangutans. Tired of waiting for Fran, she strode back to her bunk alone. She had become used to sitting and walking by herself over the past couple of weeks. So much so it sometimes startled her when someone spoke her name.

Danielle folded her arms to keep warm. The dewy grass soaked through her sneakers. She slowed down to admire a sizable spider web glistening with water beads. As she passed the mess hall, the familiar buzzing rose behind her. The Hive. What now? The giggling grew louder. Someone called out a slur that Danielle couldn't quite decipher. She was sick of feeling like every tiny move she made was projected on a drive-in movie screen. She quickened her pace and broke into a gallop. By the time she reached the bunk, she was too sweaty for her windbreaker.

Danielle opened the bunk door to find Fran sitting on a freshly made cot, fingering the gray flannel blanket bearing the iron-on Evergreen Lake patch. For once, Danielle's counselor, Lila, was in the bunk, seated beside Fran. Lila's neck now bore a triad of dark purple bruises. She had shrunk her camel-colored counselor polo shirt to the point that it tightly hugged her neat torso. Despite the cool temperature, she wore cutoff Levi's that barely covered her pink underwear. Danielle caught a glimpse of Lila's wiry blond hair poking out from the white fringe of faded denim.

Then it dawned on Danielle. The cot Fran and Lila sat atop was next to Danielle's. Danielle's bottom lip fell. She couldn't believe what she was seeing.

"That's right, Red," Fran smirked. "I got them to switch me to your bunk."

Danielle looked to Lila for confirmation.

"It's true," Lila said, in her lolling southern accent. "Gert approved the change this morning."

A friend! In her own bunk! Danielle was ecstatic. She wanted to jump in Fran's lap and throw her arms around Fran's neck. Somehow she managed to contain herself and held up her hand for a high-five. She didn't want Fran to think she was clingy.

When Lila told the bunk the news, the Simon twins had nothing to say as usual. The Five's only reaction to the announcement was to nominate Anastasia Meyer to ask— sweetly, demurely—if they could move their cots to the other side of the cabin. Anastasia explained they were working on a surprise for their newest bunk sister and didn't want it spoiled. Danielle wondered if Anastasia's parents fell for the same act.

Having the Five on the other end of the cabin proved to be a blessing. That night, Danielle and Fran stayed up late whispering about their favorite TV characters. Danielle's was Velma on *Scooby Doo*; Fran's was the drunk girl on *One Day at a Time*. Lila's bed remained empty long after Fran and Danielle's conversation trailed off. Before Fran began to gently snore, she reached across the space between the two cots and grabbed Danielle's hand. She told Danielle she wouldn't let anyone mess with either one of them anymore.

"That's a promise," Fran said, squeezing Danielle's hand.

Danielle could hardly sleep, she was so elated. Together, she and Fran would be a force to be reckoned with. With an ally sleeping under the same roof, she could deflect any insult the Five hurled her way. Fran would be at her back, ready with one of her priceless zingers. No more would Danielle have to take a hundred-yard detour to avoid one of her nemeses. No more would she have to pretend she was deaf when a girl incapable of scoring higher than a C on a geometry test called her stupid.

Danielle was already awake when the scratchy recording of the bugle playing morning reveille blared over the camp PA system at sunrise. After everyone was up, Shannon Levine sneered at Danielle and Fran, "So what were you two lovebirds gabbing about late into the night?"

The rest of the bunk was washing up in the bathroom. Shannon had worn her hair in tiny braids the day before, like Bo Derek in *10*. Now, with the braids undone and her kinked hair pointing in every direction, she looked like a mad scientist who'd accidentally blown up a beaker in her face.

A snort escaped from Danielle's nose. She sat on her cot, hugging her right leg to her chest and dangling her left over the edge. Shannon scowled and tried to smooth down her hair. Then the two girls looked at Fran, who had already begun to busy herself with her sketchbook. Any moment now Fran would put Shannon Levine in her place, Danielle was sure of it.

"Whatsamatter, greaseball? Are you mute, too?" Shannon demanded of Fran, looking disappointed that no one was taking the bait. The Simon twins emerged from the bathroom and scurried to the clothing bureau. Steffie Simon looked down at the floor as she crossed the room; Stacie looked through Danielle as if she were a glass wall.

Shannon and Danielle continued to stare at Fran, Danielle waiting for Fran to issue Shannon a verbal slap upside the head, Shannon waiting for a worthy opponent. Fran turned the page in her sketchbook and started a new drawing. Shannon scoffed and disappeared into the bathroom, tossing over her shoulder, "I guess you two chickenshits were meant for each other."

Danielle was flabbergasted. What happened to Fran's

promise the night before? Had she been lying? Talking in her sleep? Fran couldn't have chickened out—it wasn't possible. So why was she just sitting there with her mouth clamped shut?

Once Shannon was gone, Danielle said Fran's name quietly. No response. She called for Fran again, this time a bit more emphatically.

"Wait, I'm on a roll here . . ." Fran said. Her pen zigzagged wildly across the rough white paper. She still hadn't looked up.

"I don't care!" Danielle's voice sounded more high-pitched than normal. "Why didn't you say anything? What about our pact?"

Fran lifted her gaze and told Danielle not to have a hissy fit. Then Fran's voice softened as it had the night before when she seized Danielle's hand. She explained that she easily could have ripped Shannon Levine a new caboose, but she didn't want to waste her breath so early in the day.

Danielle wanted to feel relieved. But the relief wouldn't come. Instead, she felt a pinch in her abdomen, like she did right before jumping off the floating dock during swim period. She now hugged her left leg against her chest, too. Why would Fran say one thing but do another? Craig had alluded to Fran having problems. Maybe something really bad had happened to her, like getting cancer, or learning one of her parents had cheated on the other. Maybe that was why Fran sometimes changed her mind about important things, like meeting Danielle at the campfire. Or standing up to Shannon Levine just now. Maybe Fran flip-flopped because she was preoccupied. Danielle convinced herself Fran deserved the benefit of the doubt.

Fran interrupted Danielle's thoughts by asking if she could tell Danielle something private. She said it had to do with her missing campfires and switching bunks and hiding out in the art shack whenever she wanted. Danielle hopped off her cot and rushed to sit next to Fran. She gushed that whatever it was, Fran could trust her not to blab to anyone else.

"Not here," Fran said. "Meet me third period at the Oasis."

When Danielle arrived at the art shack, Craig was dancing around the room like an elf, singing along with Van Morrison at the top of his lungs. Fran was nowhere to be found. Danielle went outside and sat on the porch steps. She balanced her chin on her fists. The pinch in her abdomen returned, and the back of her neck felt hot. Was Fran just playing games with her? She went back to the bunk to look for Fran, not sure what she would say if she found her.

The trumpeting sound of a nose being blown filled the bunk. It was coming from the bathroom. Danielle tiptoed toward the toilet stalls to investigate. The middle stall was locked. She looked to the light blue concrete floor. There, Fran's suede moccasins straddled a tear-stained letter and a white envelope. The envelope had a postmark from Arizona and was addressed in cursive handwriting.

Miss Francine Flowers. That's who the letter was addressed to. Danielle couldn't imagine anyone calling Fran Francine. Francine sounded like the name of a girl who wore patent-leather shoes and pearl earrings.

A small voice Danielle didn't recognize came from the stall: "Real great presents, Ma . . ."

A turquoise-beaded bracelet slid to the floor. Then muffled sobs as Fran's right foot trounced the letter.

Danielle backed out of the bathroom as quickly as she could without her sneakers squeaking against the concrete. She was sure that whatever had Fran so upset—whatever that letter said—had something to do with the secret Fran meant to tell her at the art shack. She thought about the personal poems in Fran's sketchbooks. Fran kept them in the sticker-covered trunk at the foot of her bed. Danielle wouldn't dream of snooping through them. She'd be an idiot to risk losing her only friend in the bunk. Besides, Fran said she'd kill anyone who went behind her back, whatever that meant.

Danielle raced back to the art shack, willing Craig not to

be in the darkroom. He knew why Fran's dad had asked for special treatment for his daughter, and he might even know why Fran was crying on the toilet over a letter and gift from her mother.

"I don't know anything," Craig said, and pantomimed zipping his mouth. He sped downstairs toward the darkroom. Danielle rubbed her stomach, hesitating a moment before following him. When she reached the bottom of the stairs, the darkroom door was already shut. She banged on the door. It opened, and out came Craig, irritated, minty fresh, a partially smoked joint tucked behind his ear.

"Look, Danny Girl, don't worry about Fran so much. She can take care of herself. She's a tough little number. You should be more worried about you," he said, pointing a paint-stained finger at her breastbone.

Danielle didn't know whether to be excited that Craig had touched her and made up a nickname for her, or offended by what he just said. Why did she need to worry about herself? Sure, she was miserable at camp. But she had this place down to a science now: steer clear of the Hive, formulate escape plans for any activity that involved a ball or the water, and invent new uses for the mounds of silver glitter housed in the art shack's storeroom.

Craig nodded in the direction of the bunks and campfire pit and said, "You're a sweet kid, probably too nice for this dump. Tell your parents to send you to a different camp next summer." Then he pulled a lighter from his front pocket and shut the door.

Fran didn't bother to tell Danielle why she missed their art-shack date that morning. Even if Fran had offered an explanation, Danielle suspected it wouldn't be the full story. Instead, Fran spent most of the afternoon storming around the bunk. She wore her hiking boots so she could achieve the loudest possible clomping sound the worn wood floors allowed.

She also kept a sketchbook open on her bed. If Danielle or anyone else so much as looked at her, she'd pick up her pen, bury her head in the binding, and begin furiously scratching at the page. Sometimes she'd throw in a loud sigh or harrumph for good measure.

On the second day of her temper tantrum, Fran skipped lunch. Danielle grimaced reading the menu tacked to the bulletin board at the mess hall entrance: tuna fish, a side of macaroni salad, and grape bug juice. She did an about-face and raced back to the bunk. Fran was on her bed sketching. Danielle positioned herself on her own bed, within whispering range of Fran. She sat down gingerly, as though her gray flannel comforter was made of broken glass. She asked Fran if she wanted to talk about it. The words, "About your mother's letter, the one you were crying about in the bathroom," stuck in her throat. She wished she could say them aloud.

"Just drop it, Danielle," Fran growled. It was the first time Fran used her real name.

"I just thought you might want me to—"

Fran cut Danielle off: "What I want you to do is mind your own beeswax!"

The bunk door swung open as if on cue. The Hive shuffled in, every last one of them balancing a beehive hairdo on her head. Shannon Levine's nest of hair was the only one that wasn't lopsided. Danielle wondered if maybe they had taken the morning's auditions for the camp production of *Grease* a bit too far.

"Ah, if it isn't Thing 1 and Thing 2! Are we interrupting your little lesbo powwow?" Shannon said, her perfect cone of hair unyielding as she tilted her head.

"Can it, Janet!" Fran snarled at Shannon. "And for the record, Little Red Riding Hood is not my girlfriend, okay?" Fran jumped up and stormed outside.

"What's her problem?" Shannon Levine said to no one in particular.

"Can't you control your lezzie lover?" Tamara Grant said to Danielle.

Things were not going the way Danielle had hoped. She and Fran were hardly a unified front against the Hive. Fran's moodiness was embarrassing, her unpredictability frightening. Danielle knew she was losing Fran—and there was nothing she could do about it.

Still, The Five didn't know what was eating Fran, and Danielle did. Sort of. Which meant she had something the Five didn't. For all they knew, Fran had told Danielle everything. Danielle glanced at the sticker-covered trunk at the end of Fran's bed. She tried not to think about the secrets it contained. Her armpits moistened.

It was clear Tamara Grant planned to stare at Danielle until she got an answer.

"Why don't you give her a break? Obviously she's upset about something," Danielle said to the cluster of five cots on the other side of the bunk. The volume of her own voice and the slight tremor that had overtaken her hands surprised Danielle. She sat on them before anyone could see.

Tamara Grant was on Danielle's bed in a flash. She put her arm around Danielle's shoulder and gently dug a cherry red nail into Danielle's bicep. The overwhelming stench of Aqua Net made Danielle gag.

"And you know what that something is, don't you, lover girl?" Tamara said.

Danielle shook her head, grimacing. The smell of hair spray seared her nostrils. Tamara Grant explained there was no point hiding the truth because the Fab Five would find out anyway. Danielle suspected Tamara's quote-unquote stupendous rendition of "Sandra Dee" in her audition for *Grease* had elevated her to the position of the Five's ringleader.

Not wanting to be outdone, Shannon Levine slid across the floor in her tennis socks and joined Tamara on Danielle's cot. The two pinned Danielle down. Tamara had Danielle's wrists, Shannon had her ankles. Shannon was the smaller of the two oppressors, despite the immobile skyscraper standing tall on her head. Danielle squirmed like crazy. She tried twisting her ankles back and forth to loosen Shannon's grip on them, but it was no use. She was hogtied. In the midst of this, Steffie Simon tentatively opened the bunk door, peered in, then retreated outside.

Anastasia Meyer, Wendy Rosenthal, and Nan Finkel raced to Fran's bed and began feverishly tossing items from her trunk. A mountain of Indian shirts, comic books, magic markers, and paperbacks amassed on the floor within seconds. Anastasia Meyer was the first to grab one of Fran's sketchbooks from the trunk. She kissed the book and cracked open the binding. Danielle went bug-eyed. Her writhing grew more desperate.

"Don't! Those are private! She writes private things in them . . ." Danielle gasped. She regretted her words instantly, and panic set in. To make matters worse, Fran, who had surely heard her outburst, was now standing in the doorway. She had thrown the door open with such force the knob gouged the wall. Fran examined the carnage for a few breaths, then began screaming.

"What the hell is going on? Danielle! What did you tell?"

Danielle swallowed hard. "Nothing!" was all she could get out before someone put a dirty tennis sock in her mouth. After that, Danielle could only thrash uselessly.

"I should have known better than to trust you and that dumb-ass goody two-shoes act of yours," Fran yelled. "I see the way you look at those prima donnas across the bunk, wishing you were like them. They were right, Red. You are just a creepy little lesbo!"

All movement in the bunk stopped. Danielle lay so still she wasn't sure she was breathing. Her heart pounded in her throat and ears. Tears of exasperation squeezed from the corners of her eyes.

From the moonlight filtering into the cabin, Danielle guessed it was after midnight. It took a moment for her eyes to adjust to the dark and another for her to remember where she was. Thick rafters hovered above the cot she lay in. Dusty windows lined the room. One had a broken spider web strewn across it. The musty smell of damp wood filled her nostrils, and then she remembered.

She was still at camp.

Her chest deflated. She sunk a bit deeper under the gray flannel blanket. She felt like she was forgetting something important, something bad that had happened. Slowly, the awful memory of being pinned to the bed by Tamara Grant and Shannon Levine crystallized. Then the piercing sting behind her eyes as she replayed in her head the hateful words Fran had used to disown her.

Danielle wouldn't try to explain herself to Fran, nor would she demand an apology. There was no point. It was too late; their short-lived friendship was null and void. Besides, within an hour of berating Danielle, Fran was sitting on Tamara Grant's bed, letting Tamara polish her nails. Frosted pink, no less. And Shannon Levine was delicately braiding Fran's stringy hair, as if to console her, as Fran whimpered something about it all being her mother's fault. Shannon's beehive hairdo had finally come undone. Dangling from Shannon's wrist on a thick silver chain was a bear-claw charm the size of a nickel.

Danielle winced, remembering how Fran had squeezed her hand before falling asleep that night. Fran had promised to be her ally, her friend. It seemed so long ago, though only a few days had passed.

Danielle threw off the covers and rose to use the toilet. She shuffled in her slippers, her feet strangely heavy. The night was especially cold. She could see her breath. On her way to the stalls, she caught a glimpse of herself in the warped bathroom mirror.

Her forehead. Something was on her forehead. To her sleepy eyes it looked like an army of earwigs. On closer inspection, she saw it was black magic marker. The indelible kind. The kind that took forever to wash off. She faced the mirror head-on, shoulders rounded, chest caved.

LESBO. Someone had written LESBO on her forehead while she slept. They'd even taken pains to write it backwards, so it read correctly it in the mirror.

Danielle grabbed a washcloth and the soap bar. She worked on her forehead while using the toilet in the middle stall. The same one Fran had been crying in a couple days before. When Danielle returned to the mirror, she saw that her violent scrubbing had barely had an effect.

Danielle leaned against the chill concrete wall and slid to the floor. A numbness crept from her clenched toes to her wrinkled forehead, and she welcomed the inertia as it washed over her. She imagined this was what drowning felt like, your body going limp in a split second, so surreal as you watched yourself from the outside.

It made no difference whether she stayed up half the night trying to remove the unwanted tattoo or spent the next day wearing a wool hat. Either way, she knew that when she arrived at breakfast, no one would be saving a seat for her. And instead of five girls snickering behind her back, there would be six.

DICKEYFISH

Gloria Upper

Long winter shadows follow me as I walk from school down Madrona Drive, past Lakeside Drug Store and the Piggly Wiggly, past Epiphany Church, past ice-covered Denny Blaine Pond, and along the half-frozen muddy path between tall firs into the shady park. The other kids have gone ahead, but I don't mind. I like to look at things, go home different ways. Birds rustle in the bushes. The shriveled fallen leaves of the deciduous trees lie frosty and molding on the ground. The bare branches look brittle; if I climbed up on them they would snap. I pull a breath of delicious cold air into my lungs, hold it as long as I can, and then watch it cloud out and disappear. I stamp on ice in puddles, touch a dewy spider web, wondering if the striped spider on guard in the middle will think she has caught a fly.

At the end of the park I cross the streetcar tracks and enter a long, narrow footbridge, a high wooden trestle that crosses a deep ravine. My heart pounds as I watch for the two Irish setters who, the last time I walked home this way, ran across from the other end and waylaid me in the middle. They had barked and growled like two lions, shown their teeth, ready to snap at my legs if I moved. I'd stood there frozen, not daring to breathe until at last they ran off.

Today they don't come. I throw a stone over the edge and peer down into the woods and stream below. It's nearly dusk. My mother should be home from work by now. "You lollygagger," she'll say crossly. "What's the matter with you? Where have you been?" I'm pokey, she tells me, always dragging my feet, slow to dress for school in the morning, slow to lace the high-topped shoes I hate, slow to finish breakfast and tug on my sticky, wet galoshes. By now, my grandmother may have dressed for dinner, trying to look sober—or maybe she's still wandering the halls in her nightgown, her permed gray hair fuzzy and uncombed, glass in hand, pretending she's drinking water. I've watched her in the morning unlock the liquor cabinet, pour the gin. She thinks I don't know. Once she wet her pants at the dinner table. Sometimes she scares me. When she was drunk one time, on the maid's day off, she opened all the gas jets on the stove and nearly blew us up. Sometimes when she's working in her garden or listening to her operas on the radio, she sings and is happy; other times she's angry and mean and orders me out of her room. She hates slugs. On summer evenings, I've followed her through the garden as she chops shiny brown slugs in two with her shovel, watching their slimy insides ooze out. Once I stepped on one in my bare feet and got the gluey, sticky stuff stuck on my toes. It took a long time to get it all off that night in the bathtub.

On the other side of the bridge, weak and trembly, I grab myself, cross my legs and hop. I have to go. I'll never make it

home without wetting my pants. I look all around for the
strangers I'm not supposed to talk to and squat behind some
shrubs. I pull my coat and dress up around my waist, tip forward
to miss the underwear around my ankles. Steam and an acrid
urine smell rise; cold air creeps up my back.

I pull my underpants up, leave the shrubs, and cut through
a picket gate, past a green house, down an overgrown backyard
to the street below. A woman in a lighted kitchen window waves
at me. I wave back. The kitchen looks warm and yellow. She
must be fixing dinner.

I run down some mossy steps into the secluded garden
next to a big Tudor house, dark and quiet. The house is always
dark and quiet, as if no one is home. If I went up onto the big
covered porch, I probably could see Lake Washington and
maybe my house on the next street down, across from the park
on Lake Washington Boulevard. I'm trespassing. I've never seen
the owners here. Maybe they're on vacation in California. Last
May, on Mother's Day, I picked some daffodils here to take to
my mother. Stole them, actually. They're old people, my
mother told me—the Dickeys—don't bother them. The
garden's a fairyland, with rock gardens, Japanese maples–bare-
branched now except for a couple of tattered red leaves—
Christmas roses, a grotto with icicles and maidenhair ferns,
and a small, hidden, ice-covered pond with a little bridge.

Under the ice in the pond I see a glint of bright orange—
a goldfish! They've forgotten him. He'll freeze there all by
himself. They don't care about him. I kneel down, carefully
break the ice and lift the cold sheet off the water onto the
grass. He's alive; his bulging, sad eyes stare up at me—longingly,
I think. He must be lonely. He'll starve with no one to feed
him. His little fins are moving slightly in a circular motion; his
feathery tail hangs down sadly, waving a little. I reach into the
icy water but he swims away from my hand back under the ice
on the edge of the pond. He's all alone. He needs someone to
take care of him. I'll sneak home and get a can, come back
later and catch him, rescue him. Nobody will see me.

In my room, Dickeyfish has a flat-sided bowl with a castle he can swim in and out of, some white rocks on the bottom, and some winding green seaweed that seems to be growing. My mother has helped me fix his home and settle him in. She's not angry that I have stolen him and even seems amused at my find. Maybe she likes him. My grandmother has ventured down the hall in her nightie to admire him. She promises she won't tell the Dickeys. I sprinkle his fish food on top of the bowl every day, change his water often, put him in the sink to swim while I clean his bowl. He's a beautiful fish. I like to hold his little scaly, slimy body in my hands when I lift him back into his bowl. He knows me now, looks up at me out of the water with his round flicking eyes, swims over when he sees me. When he eats he makes little popping, sucking sounds at the top of he water. I wonder if he is happy, if he misses his pond, if the Dickeys have come back and noticed he is gone.

Then Dickeyfish starts to make the popping, sucking sounds at night when he shouldn't be hungry. I turn on the light and watch him open and close his mouth at the top of the bowl. He looks sad. I give him more food but that isn't what he wants—it's still floating there in the morning. He slurps and slurps every night when he should be sleeping. Finally I go into my mother's room and wake her up.

"I can't sleep," I tell her. "I think he might be sick."

"Well, don't wake me up," she says in her disgusted voice. "Go back to bed and ignore him." She rolls over. "He probably needs more oxygen," she says into her pillow. Her nose sounds stuffed up as if she's been crying again. "Have you changed his water like I told you?"

I start changing it every day but he still makes the sounds at night. Slurp, slurp; pop, pop.

"He's keeping me awake," I complain again. "He does it all night long."

"Maybe he's getting too much oxygen," she suggests, "or too little. Or you're feeding him too much."

I stop changing the water so often. Still he keeps making the sounds at night and in the daytime, too. I almost get to sleep, just get to the dreams, and he starts again. "Shut up," I yell at him. "What's the matter with you?" I think he looks haunted and desperate; I lie awake and worry that he can't breathe. Is he dying? What does he need? On my back in the dark, I watch the little dancing colored sprinkles I always see in the air, wondering what they are—millions of tiny bright spots of red and orange and yellow and purple, filling the dark room—and wondering when Dickeyfish will stop. I feel like I can't breathe. I remember the nightmares I used to have of being trapped in a dark tunnel and suffocating. I'd wake up crying, call out to my mother, and go into her bed.

"Can I put him in your room?" I ask my mother.

"No!" she says. "I can't have him keeping me awake! I have to get up and go to work in the morning. Just ignore him. Go back to bed."

"I can't sleep."

"You'd better figure out what to do with him, then. You'd better get rid of him."

"But I can't—"

"Do what you like with him. You'd better do something. He's your fish."

I ask some kids if they'd like Dickeyfish but no one seems to want him. My grandmother says I should take him back to the fairyland pond, but I don't dare go back there. The Dickeys might see me and know I was the thief. "Will you do it?" I ask her.

"No. What's the matter with you?" She laughs at the idea. "Of course not."

I could let him go into Lake Washington but a bigger fish or a weasel would eat him for sure. I hold his bowl over the toilet ready to pour him in; if I flush him down he will suffocate in the terrible, dark, smelly sewer. Drowning in a sewer is the worst thing I can think of. I decide to kill my fish. I carry him in his bowl down to a secret place in the garden and pour the water out. His little gills open and close as he flops on the grass and tries to breathe. Hurry, I think. I take my grandmother's shovel and bring it down on him to chop him in half. The shovel bounces off his sturdy back. I strike again harder and manage to sever his spine and cut him in two. He lies there next to the green seaweed, unmoving, the tube of his black insides showing. I'm a murderer, I think. I pick up the two halves, dig a hole in the flowerbed, put the seaweed in for him to rest on, and bury him.

No one asks me where he is that night or the next night or the next. The bowl with the little castle sits empty in my room. After we kneel for my prayers, when she says good night, I question my mother about the sprinkles: "What are they? Are they God? I can see them with my eyes closed, too," I tell her. We turn off the lights for her to look, but she still can't see them. After she's gone, cars go by on the boulevard below and make long moving shadows on the walls and ceiling. Sometimes when I get up and watch out the window at night, I think I can see Jesus in the big maple tree next door. I wonder if I could fly over there, like in my dreams. He must know what I have done. I wonder if Dickeyfish is in heaven or if he's just gone—but I'm afraid to ask.

Then the bowl and the castle disappear. My mother says my grandmother has taken them to the attic to be given away with my outgrown toys to the gardener Mr. Takahashi's children. I wish she wouldn't do that without asking me. Maybe Minaru and his sister would have liked to have Dickeyfish. I should have thought of that. When I go up to look for the bowl again, everything is gone.

I still walk home from school with the other kids. One time we took turns saying what we don't like about each other. Everyone had a fault, but they couldn't find anything wrong with me; that made me sad. Another time we had a breath-holding contest. I held my breath the longest and then everything went black and I fainted on the sidewalk right in front of Epiphany Church. Everyone just walked on. When I came to and caught up with them, they didn't believe me that I'd fainted. They thought I was faking.

My house is the farthest from school, and sometimes, when they've all left, I go through the Dickey's yard and look into the little pond to see if there's another fish. The daffodil bulbs are pushing shoots up through the dirt now, but the Dickeys never seem to be there. There's no new fish.

Mrs. Mim's Help

Sunny Speidel

Tessie was in the living room talking to the old man when she saw the familiar white van stenciled with big letters of bold orange and deep purple. The van zipped along at a good clip to the end of the cul de sac towards the Mim household. Inside, Tessie's plain face and tired body moved heavily behind the louvered windows. She felt as if the van hurtling down the street were heading for her.

The Mims lived in a pretty neighborhood developed in 1960s Kingston. Similar middle-class communities spread across the cool foothills of the Blue Mountains, back in the hopeful days after Jamaica gained its independence from England. Both the hope and the neighborhood had gone downhill, though the neighborhood less so. The Mims' white stucco house with its red tile roof sat centered in a generous yard, bordered by a rock wall and, across the driveway, an ornate, white iron gate. Today, Thomas Mim was long retired and quite frail. While they never lost sight of their class, he and Delia struggled by on his meager retirement, augmented by her present-day salary from the school.

Mrs. Mim hadn't returned. She had promised Tessie she would come back in time. Promised.

Tessie really thought Mrs. Mim was going to keep her word. The red briefcase hadn't come out in the morning when Mrs. Mim left for work. Whenever Tessie saw the red briefcase come out, she knew Mrs. Mim would have a meeting that night, even if Mrs. Mim didn't bother telling Tessie beforehand. Tessie knew. She'd expect the phone call, late afternoon, "Go ahead and give Mr. Mim supper. Open the gate for me when I come in. Turn on the front porch light and the carport light."

Tessie snuck a peek up the block just in case Mrs. Mim's blue Morris Minor might be up there. The white van pulled up next to the gate, hidden from view by an ancient bougainvillea. She shut the louvers just as the FedEx deliveryman jumped out of the van with an envelope in one hand and a clipboard in the other. He called, "Hoo hoo," at the gate.

Tessie maneuvered past the living room and dining room, back through the kitchen and into her quarters.

Mr. Mim chose that moment to call out for Tessie in his most urgent tone, because he had to go to the bathroom. "Tessie! Tessie! Tessie!"

Perhaps the deliveryman heard Mr. Mim, for he gave another shout, rattling the gate this time.

Shame and fury chased each other around the small cage of her tightened chest as Tessie hid in her dark little room.

Tessie had been playing outside with two of her sisters when her mother called her in. She was just a pickney—four or five years old—her body too small to hold the news her mother had to give her.

She'd cried hysterically the whole way to that stranger lady's house, her mother dragging her by the hand and scolding her as they lurched down the main footpath, winding between tiny houses made of corrugated zinc and scraps of construction material.

Her mother simply hadn't loved her enough to keep her. She never did love her all that much. And now Tessie was like this. Better to be invisible. You may be dead, Mummy, Tessie thought bitterly, but I still don't forgive you.

The deliveryman honked and shouted a few more times before giving up and driving off.

Still no Mrs. Mim.

Oh dear, *look* at the time. Delia Mim's delicate features twisted in distress, glancing up from the spreadsheet program to the big school clock on the wall. She moved around the office like a small bird, darting here and there, easily taking fright. She was forever setting something down and then forgetting where she'd put it. This determined how she spent a good portion of her day. Still, not many women her age were capable of meeting life at her pace. Delia had always been youthful—looking at her, you'd never guess her age—and she wouldn't tell you if you asked, either. She'd had an upsetting fall getting into the car not too long ago, still had the bruise on her hip. And it wasn't as easy as she'd thought it would be, postponing her retirement, continuing to work.

"Mrs. Smith!" she called out, greeting a businesslike, no-nonsense, middle-aged woman. "I'm off early today—I promised Tessie I'd get back before the FedEx man comes by. Well, I'm certain he has come by now, but . . ." Delia breezed past her colleague's wood- and glass-partitioned office, addressing her with an easy informality. The two had worked together the better part of twenty years. They shared values they didn't have to explain to one another. Delia paused, "You'd think I were working for her, and not the other way around at all!"

"You say a mouthful there!" replied Mrs. Smith, "You should see my phone bill; the girl makes calls as if there were no charge! I don't know where she finds the time to meet all these men."

"They do that, you know." Delia fished for her keys. "I had one once who liked the television. Sometimes I had to *ask* her to give me the remote control. Can you imagine?"

"Did you hear about Mrs. Moore? She lost her helper after seven years. The woman was having some kind of family problem, and she lived way out in Clarendon, and finally she just had to—"

"It's so difficult to find anybody these days."

"Mrs. Mim, I believe they go into computer processing."

Delia twirled the keys around her thumb, torn between feeling the need to go and enjoying the conversation. "I hired a girl I was hoping to replace Tessie with—Tessie simply has no initiative. Truth is, I don't think she's too bright, and I can't make every little decision myself! What with the way Thomas is now. So I hired this girl to work the weekend—to try her out. Well, my dear, I came home from church on Sunday, and the girl had fled! Just like that! The door unlocked and Thomas all by himself!"

"Or crime, probably," Mrs. Smith was still on her own track.

"Crime, you say? What we excel at! Some countries win gold medals—we should get the gold medal for crime." Delia jumped from subject to subject much the same way she moved around a room. "You surely don't get helpers who want to *help* any more. I do my best to get with the new attitude, but . . . Thomas forgets sometimes, still calls them servants— that won't do nowadays, will it? I must run."

"The Lord doesn't give us more than we can bear, eh, Mrs. Mim?"

"I do what I can, Mrs. Smith. I do what I can."

When Delia pulled up to the gate, Tessie was in back somewhere. Outside, at the clothesline? No, it was a bird causing the ginger lilies to move. Delia paused a moment to see if Tessie heard her come. She could use some help carrying in those heavy packages from the back. No luck.

She looked around the yard, up the block. No one who shouldn't be there. The neighbors' pack of dogs snarled through their gate. Delia could use a couple of dogs like that in her yard, but it was so expensive to feed them.

Not a month ago her friend Edith was killed in her own garden, her throat slit as she gathered a bouquet of flowers. An eighty-year-old woman, alone at her house!

Delia got out and opened the gate, sank back into the low seat, and drove up the red cement drive into the carport.

Tessie knew just where in the house she could stand to see but not be seen. She also knew she'd better open the front door—while it might be excusable to miss hearing Mrs. Mim at the front gate, it was not optional to fail to open the front door and help bring in the groceries. She unlocked the front door and turned the light on, then stood lingeringly on the front step.

"Come. Help me get these bags," Delia said, reminded again that she had to think of every single thing.

"Yes, Mrs. Mim," said Tessie in a monosyllabic voice, looking at the ground.

As Delia sailed through the door, arms laden, she glanced over at the piano. Mail was always left on the sheet music ledge. At the moment, it was completely without any FedEx envelope. "Has FedEx come by?" she asked.

"I don't know, Mrs. Mim," said Tessie, not meeting her eyes.

"Well, you would have seen it if it came by, wouldn't you, Tessie? Did you see it?"

"No, Mrs. Mim."

"Well, he hasn't come by, has he, then? You must say a thing, Tessie. Just say it straight out. Talking with you is like pulling teeth!"

"Yes, Mrs. Mim."

"I wonder where he is? He should have come by now," said Delia. "I believe I'll call."

They unloaded oranges, bananas, clear plastic bags of raw sugar, and cans of mackerel into the already full cupboards. Delia went into the living room and dropped onto the couch.

"Oh, I'm so tired this afternoon—Tessie, bring me a cold drink before I do one more thing! Do we still have any guava juice?"

"Yes, Mrs. Mim," Tessie replied, then asked if she might bathe now, before it got dark.

Servants' quarters were built into the house. Tessie's consisted of a small room with a single bed, a scarred wooden bureau, a mirror, and a high window with a grille over it that faced out at a dilapidated gardener's toolshed, nearly covered over with drooping, lavender blooms. Adjacent to the laundry room next door was her bathroom, the sole bathroom in the house built to offer only cold water.

Tessie savored her time alone. She needed to think about things that happened, think them over uninterrupted.

She let the cool water slip over her body, her thoughts taking a gloomy spiral towards home. Every one of her eleven sisters and brothers—the ones that weren't dead—had his or her own home. What hope did she have, at her age and situation, getting one now? She fingered the scar on her forearm.

That other woman is in the house that should be my house. Dear Father, let me try to count my blessings. I was lucky for my life, when I left him. But now I'm on my own, not getting any younger. What if . . . ?

Mrs. Mim did help get the savings account. She could be

okay sometimes. Tessie's account was earning interest. Except the program she signed up with called for her to go to the bank office each month to make a deposit. It was all the way downtown, a crowded and dangerous trip, where a bad man could steal the money right out of your pocket, even if you had your hand in your pocket, holding the money.

If Tessie didn't make her deposit on time each month, the account would be closed and she would have to pay a fine. This program yielded the highest interest, which was important, because she didn't have that much time left in her life to save. She'd worked with old people enough to know what happens at the end of your life, when you can't work anymore. She needed to have her own house by then.

She could never get time off to go down and make her deposits in the time required. Mrs. Mim would always say yes, you can have the time off, but whenever the day came, Mrs. Mim had some reason Tessie couldn't go.

Lord knows, you have to bear it as best you can, Tessie thought, and it not easy. It not easy.

She emerged from her shower refreshed, in clean clothes, a brief interlude in a long day starting shortly after sunrise and ending with the close of the Mim family activities in the evening.

Together Tessie and Delia gave Thomas his supper and let him go to bed. They fixed light soup and crackers for themselves—Delia directing how many crackers were allowed—and sat down to their favorite soap opera, *The Bold and the Beautiful*. There was hardly a ripple as they bid one another good night, after each had dozed off several times during the movie that followed their show.

The next morning Tessie rose when she heard Delia go into the kitchen. They boiled water and Tessie started preparing breakfast while Delia took her tea into the other room. When Tessie came into the bedroom to give Thomas his breakfast,

Delia said, "The FedEx man is to come this morning, before I leave."

The news settled in like a mask over Tessie's face.

"I hope he comes soon," continued Delia, noting her change in expression, "because I have to leave a little earlier than I said, I forgot I have to run an errand on the way in."

In silence, Tessie finished with breakfast and getting Thomas up and dressed. As she carried the empty breakfast tray into the kitchen, she noticed the red briefcase perched on the piano stool by the front door. "Cho," she thought, "me and the old man alone in this big house all the time. What a waste. And I won't get any time today, either."

As she washed up breakfast, the joyful scream of a child next door, invisible beyond the dense green maze of mango trees, made Tessie think of her own grown-up children. After her sacrifices to keep them in school, they only ever called when they wanted money. She couldn't give up her money to them! How would she ever get herself a house like that? Calling every month. They should be helping her, but none of them stepped forward. No, they didn't treat her right.

Tessie had made sure she hadn't had too many babies, not like her mother. She had the doctors cut down there. Stopped at eleven. Twelve was just too many. Didn't she know. She had been the twelfth.

As she got ready for work, Delia kept popping into the living room in various forms of undress, looking to see if she heard the FedEx van yet. She twiddled with watering the colorful orchids on her patio. Tessie picked up her nervous anxiety. Delia lost her address book in the bedding, left her dish with today's lunch on a shelf in the spare bedroom. Tessie helped her look.

In the midst of a search, the toot of the FedEx van startled them. Delia grabbed the gate key and went out to claim her package. Tessie watched them exchange pleasantries from the shadow of the front door.

She was going to have to ask Mrs. Mim, no matter what. If she didn't make her deposit today . . . She had to ask.

Delia came back in, her lips set.

"Mrs. Mim," Tessie began, "I have to make my bank deposit. Can I have two hours to go to the bank this afternoon?" She wished she'd asked last night, after *The Bold and the Beautiful.*

"Tessie, do you realize I had to *call* FedEx to get my package? I had to call them because you said they didn't come yesterday. And the driver *told me.* He told me he saw you running away from him. Honestly, Tessie, you're a grown woman! How is that any way to act? And now I have to call them back to get my package! *And* you want time off this very afternoon? Tessie, I simply can't. I have a meeting."

"But Mrs. Mim, today is the last day!" Tessie wailed, waving her arms in a wide arc, "The bank will charge me a fine! It's just two hours, I'll take a taxi! I'm no idler, I'll come right back!"

With Tessie tagging behind her, Delia snatched the red bag off the stool and took it into the dining room. In her annoyance, she fumbled its clasp, opened it and began stuffing a wad of papers into the bag. "I might've had time this morning . . . *if* you'd given me any kind of notice, *if* I didn't have to think of every single thing, and *if* I didn't have to be here to get my FedEx package. But I did have to be here this morning, didn't I?"

"Mrs. Mim! I tried two times before, but you—"

"Damn it, Tessie! Lord knows I try to put up with your shortcomings, but I *won't* put up with this attitude! What good *are* you?! You don't even know how to *read*! What can you do for me anyway? You can't even sign the FedEx form!"

Tessie's face crumpled. "I wouldn't be working *here* if I knew how to read!"

"Oh, take your tears into your own room, I need to answer

the phone," said Delia, cutting it off mid-ring as she picked up the receiver. "Good morning, Lillian. Will you be there this afternoon? Might be late? Call me at the office," and here she dropped into a stage whisper that could be heard two houses down the block, "Certainly don't bother to leave a message here," she adopted a girlish, gossipy tone, "Tessie can't *read*, you know. No, you didn't *know*? You've left your *number*? And I've called back? Well, you were lucky my dear, she had a good memory that day. It doesn't extend to every day, let me tell you!"

Tessie felt like wet clay, sitting on the side of her tiny bed. She wished Mrs. Mim hadn't seen the tears. She wished a lot of things. Her hands curved into fists as she thought it, "Why, Mummy? I wasn't the oldest. I wasn't the youngest. That woman you sent me to never loved me. She never loved me. She never even let me go to school!"

"Tessie," Delia called from the kitchen.

Tessie wiped her face and paused in the dark room behind her closed door a moment before she stepped out into the washing room and, through the doorway, stood stone-faced before Mrs. Mim. "Yes'm."

"I'm leaving now. Come shut the gate for me, please? If I don't return in time this evening, go ahead and let Thomas go to bed after supper, but make sure he takes his medication first."

They walked out through the yard together, and Tessie shut the gate behind Delia, who gave a little wave out the driver's side window. But her charm wasn't working on Tessie, who latched the gate without response.

It was dark when Delia pulled in. Tessie turned on the outside lights and crossed the yard to open the gate. "Crossing a dark yard is pure trouble, even if it is Mrs. Mim's yard," she grumbled to herself. When she saw Mrs. Mim watching her from the car, she realized Mrs. Mim was nervous, too.

What a relief to see the light come on and Tessie crossing the yard to open the gate so Delia didn't have to get out of the car and walk through that big shadow cast by the ponciana tree. The whole yard was full of shadows—the hibiscus, ixora, and poinsettia shrubs all offered sinister shelter between the carport and front door.

One time she'd seen a mongoose dart out from the sedge and run across the walkway, dodging into the shelter of the big ferns. Although a bite from a mongoose was nothing compared to the bite of a bad man's gun.

The dangerous place Kingston had become! She actually took a bit of comfort from Tessie's bulky frame.

Once inside, Delia dropped an armload of notebooks on the bed and handed Tessie a bag of groceries to put away while she went to greet Thomas. "I'm just exhausted—the meeting seemed never to end! I must say, Mrs. Jackson *warmed* to her topic! And she's a talkative woman under the best of circumstances!"

"When you go back into the kitchen, Tessie, put some milk on for cocoa, and I'll be out to finish it up, I simply must get off my feet for a minute." Then, as she noticed Tessie's sullen hostility, she remembered the upset that morning. Boy, Tessie could hold a grudge. Delia couldn't understand how she could be so moody. "And put enough on for yourself, too," she added.

Delia didn't see the piece of paper on the dining room table until she was walking back from the kitchen with her cocoa. The letters and numbers were large and childlike. Some of them were written backwards, and none ran on a straight line. She could just make out a misspelled name and a tumbling telephone number.

Tessie was already in the living room, getting ready to sit on the spare green chair she was allowed to sit in. She set her cocoa on the coffee table. She set Mrs. Mim's handpainted English teacup on the dark wood side table next to the

overstuffed floral chair Mrs. Mim favored. Tessie carefully gave
no indication she'd seen Mrs. Mim looking at the piece of paper
on the table.

Delia sat down, heaved a sigh and took a sip of cocoa. That
she fell into a moment of silent contemplation went unnoticed
as an advertisement for a locally made soft drink, featuring a
loud dancehall soundtrack, played on the television.

"Well, Tessie," she mused, "I suppose I could ask one of
the teachers up at school to come by once a week and teach
you to write. Mrs. Smith might know the right person."

"Yes, mum," said Tessie. The room was dark around the
edges, and the lizards that lived behind every mirror and
framed picture inched their way out, hopeful for fat bugs. Delia
glanced sideways at her. In the flickering light of the television,
she studied a shift in Tessie's expression. She saw a sensitivity
around the eyes, almost imperceptible. Tessie undid the clip
fastening her hair.

"Tessie," said Delia, "I feel for some biscuits. Get some for
me from the kitchen, nuh?"

Tessie heaved herself out of the chair. Her sandals slapped
on the tiles as she walked into the kitchen and put a half dozen
biscuits onto a small plate. She returned and wordlessly set the
plate on the table next to Mrs. Mim.

The theme music from *The Bold and the Beautiful* came up
on the TV. They settled comfortably into their chairs.

THAW

Jason Herman

The next evening, when Jacob returned to Sneva's house, he saw that he had forgotten to lock the door. It was wide open and snow had blown into the garage. He froze, horrified. The dog was not there. A knot tightened in his chest and he ran outside to check the backyard, but he knew the dog was gone. The yard was a wasteland of white snow.

He wanted to cry, but he knew that he had to find the dog as quickly as possible, before it froze to death, if it hadn't already. He ran out to the street, cupped his hands around his mouth, and yelled as loudly as he could: "Maxwell! Maaax-welll!" He stopped and listened. The only sound was the heavy acceleration of cars spinning their wheels, high-centered in two feet of snow. He tried calling again, but it was snowing hard now, and his voice was muted by the soft, insulating layer that covered everything around him.

He started to walk down the block, then began to run, his feet slipping on the compact layer of ice beneath the light snow. His eyes scanned the frozen yards around him for any sign of the dog, and he continued to yell, his voice cracking and breaking. He began to sweat from the running, and tears streaked his face. He slipped and fell, landing sideways in the deep snow. He lay there for a moment, overwhelmed, then pounded the ground with his fists and got up again, running.

He searched the neighborhood for two hours. No sign of the dog. It was completely dark, nearly nine o'clock, when he gave up and started heading home. His cheeks and his ears were bright red, his hair wet from the melting snow. He thought of the dog, half-frozen, hungry, and wandering the streets alone. He thought of the old man and how he would have to tell him that he, Jacob, had been careless, stupid—that he had done exactly what the old man told him not to do, and the dog was gone because of it.

A car's headlights lit up the street ahead of him, and he moved to the side of the road to let it pass. He watched, blinded for a moment, as the car sped easily past him on the plowed road. After it passed, Jacob remained standing there. The lights had revealed something lying in the snow on the opposite side of the street.

He walked slowly across the street, knowing exactly what he would find, even though he had seen only something brown, indefinite, half-buried under the snow. He found the dog there, on the far side of the snowbank that had been left by the plow. The dog lay on its side, snow covering most of its body except for a few patches the wind had blown away. Its brown and white fur was crusted with tiny balls of snow. Its face had been torn open and a large flap of skin was pulled back over its eye, so that Jacob could see all of its teeth and its jawbone. Dried blood, almost black in the cold and the dark, stained the fur around its ears. Jacob took off a glove and brushed some snow away from the dog. It was frozen solid.

Jacob fell back against the snowbank and closed his eyes, but he couldn't hold back the tears. There was nothing he could do. He wanted so badly to go back to the night before, to just do that one thing differently, to pay a little more attention to what the old man had said. He walked through everything he had done in his mind, from giving Maxwell his food to letting him out to the backyard, to putting the dog back in the garage and shutting the door behind him when he left—but this time, in his mind, he locked it. He imagined himself home now, in his bed, sleeping, instead of out here, lying in a snowbank next to a frozen, bloody dog whose death he was responsible for. He thought of the driver who had run over the dog, and his body tingled with rage. Whoever it was hadn't even stopped, hadn't even bothered to find out whether the muffled thump they had heard was someone's companion, someone's friend. Then Jacob thought of Maxwell, dying in the snow, whimpering, bleeding, lonely. He cried for the dog's sufferings, for his own, for the old man's. Then he got up, kicked some snow over the dog, and walked home, crying. He didn't know what to do.

For the next few days, he couldn't concentrate on anything. Even when he wasn't thinking of the dog or the old man— when he was sitting in class or watching television at home—a heaviness and a tightness in his chest reminded him of some grief, some fear not far from the surface. He thought about the old man's cold house, he imagined him coming home, expecting to hear Maxwell whining, but hearing nothing and walking into the garage to find it empty, lifeless. He tried to imagine what the old man would do. Would he cry? Would he walk next door and demand an answer from Jacob?

At times Jacob lost himself so deeply in thinking about the situation that, for a moment, it didn't seem so bad. How upset could the old man be? After all, it was only a dog, not a human being, not his son or daughter. Jacob would feel relieved and forget about it, but then, only minutes later, the weight of his anxiety would slide back onto him, all the heavier for his having briefly forgotten it.

He didn't know exactly what kind of response he feared from the old man: anger, or tears, or a heart attack. He couldn't imagine the old man being violent, or even getting terribly worked up either to mourn or to punish. He didn't expect, even, that the old man would fail to pay him. All he feared, all he found himself unable to face or even imagine, might be simply but devastatingly realized in a dismissive wave of the hand, a slow shaking of the head, a sigh, or a snort. He feared, above all, the old man's disappointment. He could not tell him. He could not.

Sneva ordered a scotch on the plane ride back to Spokane. He didn't usually drink during flights, but he felt angry, let down, as if the world owed him a drink. The week at his daughter's had been just what he expected: a parade, an artificial propping-up intended to make him feel that life wasn't all that bad. They took him to see the city, and they were frozen and miserable walking the downtown streets. They took him out for steak, for seafood, for crème brûlée and coffee—they drank wine every night. He knew they were trying hard to please him, and it only made him angry with them because it depressed him. Even the little things his daughter had done around the house to make him feel comfortable irritated him. He had made a sarcastic remark when he found that she had ordered the paper just for his visit. "I stopped reading it," he had said. "I don't want to expose myself to all that pain and suffering." He didn't touch it all week.

Sneva turned out the light above him and lowered his seat back. All the harsh words he had spoken, all the little daggers he had thrown at his daughter, who he knew was only trying to love him, now repeated themselves with ugly clarity in his mind. He loved her—God, he loved her. And he hated himself for the way he had treated her. But even now, he felt justified—regretful, but justified. What else could he do? His life was bleak, it was painful, it was dark, and no week away could change that. But he felt that now, coming home, it was even more bleak. That he had only widened the gulf between himself and the only person he still loved.

He thought for a moment about calling her on the in-flight phone that was nested into the seat in front of him. He even got out his credit card and tapped it lightly on the plastic beverage tray, considering. But what would he say? I'm sorry? For what? Would she even understand? Maybe she hadn't even noticed his bitterness, maybe she would have no idea what he was talking about. He was probably exaggerating the whole thing. He put the credit card back in his wallet and tried to stop thinking about it.

The plane had begun its descent over Montana, and Sneva gazed out the window on the tiny communities below whose lights cast a milky glow onto the white landscape. He watched as houses and neighborhoods gave way to mountains with frozen, snowy summits that shone in the moonlight. He imagined the windblown loneliness a man would feel standing on top of one of those mountains on a night like this. And he watched as the mountains gave way and, again, tiny houses and streets salted the darkness with light.

The plane was low enough now that Sneva could see Christmas lights on some of the houses. Colored bulbs traced the outline of snow-covered roofs, and on a few he saw a dense color patch that he took to be a glowing Santa Claus or a reindeer. One house, in particular, caught his attention and held it. It was a simple display: a string of white lights spread across an entire roof in the outline of a cross. A thin cloud was passing over the ground below, and it made the lines of the cross soft, indefinite.

It reminded Sneva of something, but he didn't know what. He ordered another scotch to jog his memory. Yes, he remembered, that was it: the simple, white cross that had hung

in the Lutheran church where he had spent two years of
Saturdays in confirmation classes as a boy. The cross was thin
like this one, almost frail. It had hung from the wall, leaning
out toward the congregation at an angle, ready, it seemed, to
fall on the pulpit at the first sign of unbelief. Sometimes, on
those Saturday afternoons, Sneva had hoped it would fall. How
he had despised the simpleton who taught those classes: the
ugly, yellow-toothed man who spent two whole Saturdays
explaining why infants who die without salvation must by
necessity be cast into hell. Sneva had entered those classes with
genuine belief and, two years later, had made a public
profession of faith in a religion that he privately scorned.

Yet Sneva's memory of those Saturdays was not entirely
without redemption. His father had been away at the war,
stationed on a battleship somewhere in the Atlantic. But
his uncle had spent those Saturdays with him. His father's
brother, Frank, whose own children were already grown,
had walked with Sneva to the church each week and picked
him up in the afternoons as well. Sneva remembered walking
in the mornings, stopping at Dean's grocery, where Frank
would buy them both fresh donuts. And then, after class,
Frank waiting for him outside the building, leaning against
the wall, smoking a pipe. They would walk into town, where
his uncle would stop at the post office or get a haircut or
spend half an hour in the sporting goods store, showing
Sneva which lures were catching the fish that season. Then
Sneva's mother would ask Frank to stay for dinner, and the
three of them would sit around the table until late in the
evening, telling stories, talking about Sneva's father.

Once, Frank allowed him to skip confirmation altogether
and took the boy fishing. He let Sneva use his knife to clean
the fish, teaching him where to make the cut in the belly and
how to tear out the guts with one swift pull. Afterwards, they
had gone to Frank's house so they could clean up and arrive
home at the proper hour. It had been their secret.

Sneva had not thought about his uncle much since then,

but he realized now that he longed for him. It occurred to Sneva that he had learned more about love—about self-sacrifice—from Uncle Frank than he had learned from those confirmation classes, from the church itself. Surely the church—surely institutionalized religion—had gotten it all wrong. It seemed to him that now, especially now, he could understand the cross. Lonely, afflicted, suffering, abandoned. Yes, he convinced himself, he still believed in Jesus: a Jesus who was misunderstood, a Jesus who was betrayed and lonely, a Jesus who, in spite of his suffering, loved those around him, a Jesus who made the ultimate sacrifice for his love. Religious fanatics and zealots had turned Jesus into a god, into a means of salvation, all too willing, themselves, to let him do the work. But that was not the message of the cross. The message of the cross was self-sacrifice, a deliberate giving away of oneself.

A tingle ran up Sneva's spine, all the way to his lips, which were numbed slightly from the scotch. He felt a kind of electricity buzzing throughout his body. He raised his seat up and looked around at the people sleeping. He wanted to shout, to wake them up. He had found it. He would give himself to the boy. He smiled and shook his head in wonder that he had not thought of it before. All these years, next door to him the boy had been without a father, while he had sat alone, mourning the loss of his wife and son. The boy was only twelve years old—he needed a father, a mentor, a guide. Sneva could offer him that. And the irony of it, the sheer, silly irony of it, was that this fathering, this giving of himself, was the key to the happiness that had for so long eluded him, the happiness he had given up believing in.

When he got home, Sneva still felt the current in his veins. He dropped his suitcase in the hall and went out to the garage wearing his coat and hat. It was odd that Maxwell had not barked—perhaps he was asleep. But when Sneva opened the door, the dog was not there. He checked the outside door: locked. The garage was warm, so the door hadn't been left open recently. He walked outside, scanned the yard, spoke the dog's name, and went back in.

Perhaps the boy had taken Maxwell home for the night. He hadn't told the boy not to, and maybe it wasn't such a bad idea. Even dogs got lonely. In the kitchen, a message blinked red on the answering machine—the boy, he thought. But it was not the boy. Maxwell had been spotted on the side of the road by a motorist. Struck by a car. The city had sent someone to collect the carcass. Phone number on the tags.

Sneva stood there in the unlighted kitchen. The loss was so sudden, but he felt the fullness of it in an instant. The silent house was saturated in it. He pictured Maxwell lying in the snow on the side of the road, bloody, lifeless. He tried not to think of the dog's suffering, and he tried to hear the click-clack of the dog's toenails on the tile floor of the kitchen. He walked outside again and saw that Maxwell had dug his way under the fence. Even in the snow, the dog had found a way to get out—relentless to the very end. The old man sobbed once, deeply. Then he thought of the boy.

It was clear the boy had left the door open, but Sneva was not angry. Yes, it was the boy's fault. Yes, he had been careless. But he was a boy—a boy without a father. This would change nothing. Sneva would forgive him. He forgave him even now.

The next day was a Saturday, and at ten o'clock—the appointed time—Jacob again walked up Sneva's driveway. The snow had begun to melt the day before, then frozen overnight, and Jacob's boots crunched and cracked the ice. He was heavy with guilt. The night before, a rash had broken out across his stomach.

He knocked on Sneva's door and for a second considered flight—sprinting across Sneva's frozen front yard and back to the safety of his own home. But he knew he had to face the old man eventually.

Sneva opened the door and cast a stony, expressionless look

at the boy. His face seemed paler, more wrinkled to Jacob than it had before. He stepped aside to let the boy in, but said nothing.

Jacob avoided the old man's eyes, keeping his gaze fixed upon the brown tile in the hallway.

"About Maxwell," he began, "I don't know what happened."

The old man remained silent. He was waiting for the boy's confession—then he would break the stoicism and lavish him with mercy.

"Someone must have gotten in somehow, I—"

"Eh?" the old man snorted involuntarily.

"I don't know." Jacob shook his head. He had not planned to lie, but when he saw the old man's granite face, he retreated. He couldn't let him down. He couldn't let him down. "I locked the door. I . . . Someone must have gotten in. Someone must have broken in."

Sneva was shocked, fumbling. He took a step backwards.

"That's impossible, son." He strained his eyes to look at the boy, concentrating, trying to comprehend.

"I know, I know. I don't understand it. I locked the door behind me. I locked it every night."

"It's okay, son. I know you left it unlocked. It's okay. Maxwell was hit by a car. But I'm not angry with you. Just tell me the truth." His eyes had grown large, desperate—his voice was pleading. He felt the boy slipping away from him.

Jacob hesitated—he considered changing course. But then the old man would know that he lied. That he killed the dog and lied. He couldn't go back now—he had insisted on his innocence, he had committed. He felt himself dividing, almost as if he were leaving his own body. He wanted to reach out for the old man's forgiveness, but he could not. He felt as if he were watching himself from deep inside his own body. Inside, he was crying, screaming, confessing—this outside boy standing in the hallway lying, this was not him.

"I locked the door." His words were flat now, his eyes glossy and unfocused. He continued to stare at the floor.

Sneva looked at the boy, horrified. It was out of his hands, beyond his comprehension. The boy's failure, the boy's carelessness, even the boy's malice he could have forgiven. But this was beyond him. The stubborn, stupid insistence—the sheer illogic of it—Sneva could not gloss over. How could he forgive what had not even been confessed? He shook his head, took a twenty dollar bill from his wallet and handed it to the boy, saying nothing.

The boy left, and Sneva shut the door behind him. He stood there, stunned, impotent. It had happened so quickly. His sacrifice had been snuffed out. For a moment, he considered going after the boy, to challenge him, to force an admission, to thrust his mercy upon him. He remembered he was lonely, and he longed for the boy. But he did not move, he could not move. After a few minutes, he lay down on the couch and slept.

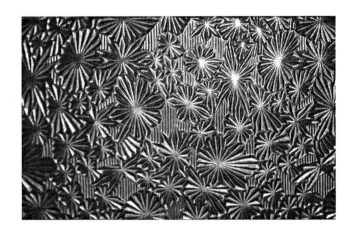

GREEN TIME

Julie Schickling

The place was called Green Time. Lily had seen a sign for it somewhere, some really public place, maybe Stazione Termini. She remembered that the sign was not enticing, it looked plain and sleazy simultaneously. Green Time.

But Rhonda wanted to go, and she insisted that Lily go too. And Lily wanted to go out, she loved to dance, but she had doubts about this place. There were certainly some great clubs in Rome, but she didn't think that Green Time was one of them.

They were back at the pensione. Lily was attempting to dress privately behind the armoire door. Rhonda reclined in lacy bra and panties on the bed. She was entertained by Lily's embarrassment. "Lily," she teased. "What are you doing back there?" She leaned up on an elbow, trying to see better. Lily blushed, holding her blouse against her chest. Rhonda sighed and looked up to the ceiling. "Heavens," she said. "You are unbelievably prim."

Lily turned away, bending her head as if looking for something. A delicate wedge of hair emerged from beneath the precisely cropped line just above her neck and trailed in a fine fuzz downward. She spoke into the armoir. "Compared to what?"

Rhonda didn't seem to hear. She lay back down and mused, "What should I wear?" Her voice was an incantation to pleasure. She languished in a brief sensual torpor and then rose like Venus to the wardrobe, her practiced arm extended to flick through the hangers of her adornments.

Lily was still buttoning her blouse as Rhonda began to pull out various small filmy items and hold them up to herself. Unexpectedly, Lily experienced a disturbing wave associated with Rhonda's proximity and sought some distance across the room. She noticed the long curtains drifting in the soft breeze coming from the balcony. They reminded her of a slow dance. She felt a vague sense of foreboding.

"Do you like this outfit?" Rhonda said.

Lily peeked out of the corner of her eye. She wanted to prepare herself for whatever state of nakedness Rhonda might be in. She told herself that she should have remembered Rhonda's proclivities, considering various sightings and encounters on campus back home, but no. When they had run into each other at the train station, they had been like long-lost friends, destined to share a room together for the week before their separate study programs began. Now Lily felt stifled by the volume of Rhonda's extroverted voluptuousness in their chaste twin-bedded room.

She turned her head to see Rhonda's considerable cleavage festooned on either side by huge pink ruffles on a sleeveless cotton shirt, offset by a tight black miniskirt. Rhonda admired herself unabashedly; her full and pinkened lips hovered close to the mirror, rehearsing a kiss.

Lily resumed the banter that had been escalating since they moved into the small room. "My God," she said. "Why don't you just carry a For Rent sign?"

Rhonda laughed. "I take that as a Yes," she said.

Lily said, "You take everything as a Yes."

She felt Rhonda's gaze upon her from the mirror. Rhonda's eyes traveled down her blouse and tight new jeans. "You could at least undo another button," Rhonda pronounced, turning back to the mirror.

"Perché non," she continued, shrugging, palms up. "Why not?" She tilted her chin over her shoulder so that she could inspect her backside in the mirror.

Half an hour later they stood outside of Green Time. The entrance was a generic glass door with dull metal trim, suburban and cheap, tacked into ancient blocks of stone that had been dragged there centuries ago. Muted rhythm pulsed the glass. Rhonda pulled open the door and disco music tumbled out upon them like a runaway machine. They entered through a barrage of staccato eighth notes.

A small vestibule ejected them into a horizontally expansive room, where they were sprayed by ellipses of light from a mirrored ball that spun above the dance floor. Intermittently the club seemed dark as a cave. They stood together for a moment while their eyes adjusted to the gloom. Unknown observers encircled them in steamy depths.

Lily became aware of a thin, dark-suited man exhaling smoke in a flume that veiled his face; his eyes beamed on them, reflecting pinpoints from the ember of his cigarette. Lily sensed some kind of hunger coiled up in him. Without thinking she grabbed Rhonda's fleshy elbow. Rhonda patted and then held her hand, and Lily wasn't sure if she'd rather be abandoned in this place of devouring eyes or connected to the force field of Rhonda's physicality.

Rhonda led them closer to the dance floor, then stopped and posed: chin up, shoulders back, right hand extended, pinky out. She surveyed the room and squeezed Lily's hand.

"I like the one by the door," she said out of the corner of her mouth. Lily could hardly hear her over the music; she turned to see what had transfixed Rhonda like a pointer dog and saw the man with the cigarette now staring back at Rhonda. His face was momentarily tinged a lurid blue.

"Oh my God, I can't believe you're serious. He's awful."

Rhonda was still staring at him, a funny smile playing on her lips. "Maybe," she said. "I kind of like awful men though."

"I hate this," Lily said.

Rhonda patted Lily's hand again before she disengaged herself. She said, "You'll be fine," as she wafted away. Soon Rhonda was on the dance floor with the awful man, his eyes staring into hers. He had one hand grasping her posterior as if it were a basketball. His other arm was draped over her shoulder, his fingers dangling limply, holding a fresh cigarette. Its wan smoke meandered into the haze.

Lily turned away. "Why did I let her talk me into this?" she said to herself. The man was probably much older, at least thirty-five. She scanned the room in search of refuge. The bar seemed a good place to start; she could at least obtain the distance and sedative qualities of alcohol. She decided to make her way across the stone floor tiles without stepping on the cracks. This minimized the possibility of eye contact, since she would have to look mostly at the floor.

When she arrived at the bar, Lily stopped to collect herself. She set her purse on the polished wood surface and smoothed her dark hair with both hands, as if she had just surfaced from underwater. She ignored the several men leaning on the counter and raised her eyes to the bartender. He faced her across the bar and inclined his ear toward her. She whispered into it, "Amaretto." He put an inch into a rotund shot glass and handed it to her.

She extracted some lira notes from her purse and set them

down on the countertop. Her eyes made random, furtive glances as her fingers scooted the bills toward the bartender, seeking a tacit alliance. Forsaking the assortment of coins he returned, she stood there, sipping at the liqueur. She felt its medicinal burn travel down her throat, making its presence known throughout her system, soothing her stomach. Though she rarely smoked, she wanted a cigarette. Conveniently she was carrying Rhonda's pack in her purse. She pulled one out and instantly a flame appeared to light it. The man holding the lighter was like a gargoyle, motionless, gazing at her intently. She raised the cigarette to her lips as he positioned the flame, waiting for her to inhale. She took a short drag and he popped the lighter shut.

She turned away, refusing to acknowledge him further. He continued to stare; she felt her neck becoming stiff. The man would not give up. She remembered a phrase she had heard Rhonda use dismissively. Exhaling, she said distinctly yet without looking at him, "Vai via." To her surprise he moved away.

She looked out onto the dance floor. Random light flashed on several couples who were oblivious to the fast beat, swaying to their own rhythm. In each pair, the man had his arm drooped over his partner's shoulder, cigarette streaming, identical with the others. They reminded Lily of oil derricks, their arms like booms, pumping away. Further back a dark-hued cluster of young people undulated. They looked both wholesome and sophisticated, the men in sport jackets and slacks, the women in formfitting, low-cut evening gowns.

Lily was beginning to perspire in her Qiana shirt. Worse, she feared that she was inappropriately dressed. Still, she thought that her ensemble, purchased that afternoon on the Via del Corso, would be the height of chic at home. Rhonda was on a different plane: her style of dressing knew no boundaries.

Lily spotted them, Rhonda and the awful man, coming towards her; he had his arm around Rhonda's waist and was steering her. Lily was feeling the warmth of the liqueur; it was like an anchor. She took a long drag off the cigarette and tilted

back her head, exhaling through her nose. She decided that
Rhonda was quite lovely in the intermittent dark of the disco
lights, her flamboyance muted. She pictured her in a sleek
shift with her hair in a demure bun: a prim Rhonda with
unplumbed depths.

"You've got the right idea," Rhonda said in a husky voice.
"A drink." She stood close to Lily and spoke over the music
while she held the man's arm, pulling him towards them. "This
is Giorgio." His melancholic eyes were huge in his thin face.

Lily nodded at him; she said, "Giorgio." She pointed to
herself and said, "Lily."

He pointed to her and repeated, "Lily." His thin mustache
was dyed and waxed; its two halves rode his lips like military
insignia.

She raised her drink in salute and said, "Drink."

He laughed and repeated, "Drrrink."

"Quite the linguist," she said to Rhonda, who winked back
and slithered her tongue snake-like. Lily rolled her eyes with
distaste. She finished the last of her liqueur and set the glass
down on the bar. Giorgio said, "Un altro?" and she replied,
"Grazie, amaretto per favore."

"Certo." He nodded and Lily couldn't tell if he was smiling.
She detected an arrogance beneath his civility. He moved away
to initiate a formal transaction with the bartender.

"Now I'm stuck here for another drink," she said.

Rhonda said, "He's really not so awful. He has a friend too."

"Oh God. I knew there was a catch to that drink."

Rhonda grabbed Lily's hands and leaned against her as she
spoke into Lily's ear.

"Lily." Her voice was coaxing. "Relax. Come on. Have some
fun."

Lily had been considering leaving Green Time right that
minute, but she decided that if Rhonda really wanted her to
stay, she could endure a little longer. Giorgio was already
coming toward them holding two drinks. Another man followed
him with two more drinks.

"All right," Lily sighed. She twisted her neck to avoid breathing in Rhonda's face. "If you say so."

She stepped slightly behind Rhonda as Giorgio staked his claim. With a drink in each hand he guided his arm around Rhonda's waist. Magically they entwined, like a candelabra, sweaty glasses upraised.

Giorgio turned to present Rhonda to his friend, a compact man with dark blonde hair that bristled up like a baby brush. He had a big smile and deep dimples in his cheeks. His collar splayed out like two white flags from his shirt, which was parted at the top, revealing some robust chest hair. Lily could tell he was American before he said a word.

She looked over Rhonda's shoulder; they stood opposite the friend whose name, Giorgio said, was Bruce.

There was an awkward moment while Bruce stood there with his hands encumbered and then remembered that he had brought a drink for someone, who could it be? He was still staring at Rhonda. Giorgio interrupted, pulling Lily forward and saying her name.

"Piacere, Brrruchay," Lily said. The amaretto was working. "Is that the Italian form of Brutus?"

Bruce appeared not to hear. "Ciao Lily," he said, dragging out the words like a weary child as he relinquished the drink to her. When Lily thanked him he said, "My pleasure," and then suddenly turned and looked at her sideways with one eye, as if through a magnifying glass. She was surprised to hear him mutter "Amaretto" in a snide voice. Lily stood rigidly. She looked away from him, her ears distended, scanning for signals.

Then Rhonda began to strain toward the dance floor. "I love this song! It's great! Come on, Giorgio! Dance with me!"

There was some confusion about where to put their drinks. Rhonda led them all to a narrow bar somewhat sheltered from the dance floor. She put down her drink and turned to them.

· "Lily! Bruce! Come on and dance with us!" She pulled Giorgio by the hand.

Lily took a mouthful of amaretto, then she and Bruce trailed behind them, avoiding each other's gaze. Their bodies began motions that seemed unrelated to themselves. They faced each other as if they were dancing together but were not allowed to acknowledge it. Meanwhile Rhonda had pushed Giorgio across the floor and was writhing against him provocatively.

In the segue before the next song, Bruce dropped his arms and pivoted off the dance floor. Lily stood there. At the other edge of the floor, Giorgio collapsed and melded onto Rhonda.

Lily considered alternatives. She wanted to leave, but she wanted to tell Rhonda first. She could ask Bruce to tell her, but she didn't want to speak to him. She might as well finish her drink and wait for Rhonda and Giorgio to come back.

Bruce was sitting at a small round table near where they had left their drinks. He was smoking a cigarette. Lily was surprised when he turned to welcome her, his big dimples activated. She decided to give him another chance and sat down with her amaretto. The acoustics of the spot seemed more favorable for conversation.

Bruce glanced toward the motionless mass that was Giorgio and Rhonda. "That Rhonda's something else," he said. "Must be hard to travel with such a good-looking woman."

Lily's nostrils flared. She said, "I find it amusing."

Was he mean, or just insensitive? The distinction interested her for some reason.

"Anyway we aren't traveling together. We're sharing a room for a few days, and then I'm going to Florence."

He turned back to her, his pale and protuberant eyes unblinking. "I didn't think she was your type. What are you doing in Florence?"

Her type? Lily felt a trapdoor somewhere near that was about to open. She decided to ignore it. "I'm going to school, studying art history."

"Oh," he said, "Art history. That fits. You have that look."

She didn't know whether to be flattered or not. He seemed intrigued with her momentarily, or with some image he had in his mind.

"That look," she repeated. She took out a cigarette and Rhonda's lighter, willing him not to give her a light, not to even think of it.

"You know, studious." He made no attempt.

"Thanks," she said. She didn't care what he thought. She lit her cigarette.

"Ethereal," he said.

"I like that better." She exhaled.

"I thought so," he said.

So presumptuous. He was not to be trusted.

"What about you?" Lily asked. "What are you doing in Rome?"

His demeanor became vague, his aura dimmed. "Oh," he said, "my father's with the embassy. I've lived all over the world."

Lily wasn't sure if she believed him. "I wouldn't have guessed," she said.

He remained impenetrable. "Good," he said. "I don't like to be obvious."

She felt herself lured into his obscurity. His evasions were like breadcrumbs on a path to some revelation.

"Do you live with your parents?" she asked. He seemed to be close to her age, somewhere in his young twenties.

"I travel a lot," he said. He would not be pinned down.

They were sipping steadily. Lily felt the enclosure of alcohol descend upon them like a net. The music and lights were a carnival backdrop. She looked out and saw Giorgio's profile tilted up to the ceiling, his ubiquitous smoke rising up like steam. Rhonda clung to him like an exhausted swimmer.

"How do you know him?" Lily said. "Giorgio." She looked back at Bruce. She wasn't sure if she saw his face soften with something like affection.

"Giorgio," he repeated. "He worked for my father. I've known him since I was a child."

He gazed away, elsewhere, excluding her. Lily drifted along in the cottony gauze of atmosphere, content in her fog, wondering if Giorgio had worn a uniform.

Suddenly Bruce touched the top of Lily's hand with one finger and moved his face close to her. She could feel his breath as his eyes fastened onto hers. "Giorgio taught me everything." He withdrew then, as if to deny what had just occurred.

"Let's have another drink," he said. He signaled a man she hadn't noticed who was apparently a waiter. The man nodded.

"So," Lily said, regaining her breath. She wasn't sure what was making her dizzy, the amaretto or the conversation. She wanted to change the subject. "What is 'Green Time,' anyway?" she asked. "Does it mean anything?"

"'Green Time,'" Bruce said, "it means Now. Green light. Go."

"Where?" said Lily.

He made no reply. He stared out at the dance floor, breathing through his mouth.

They were well into the next round of drinks when Rhonda and Giorgio joined them at the table. Giorgio's tie was loosened and some buttons were undone on his shirt, though his jacket remained correct as ever. Rhonda played with his fingers on the table, conversing with him in monosyllables. Lily perceived dimly that Giorgio's hands were small, not much bigger than Rhonda's, and his fingers were thinner, and pointy, with fine black hair between each joint. Her sudden queasiness caused her brain to lurch into focus. It was time for her to go.

There was a gloom congealing. Bruce was drinking too fast. The music had become tinny and extraneous. Lily wanted to get Rhonda's attention, to tell her that she was leaving.

Bruce had become a tentacled swamp; his vaporous presence loomed. No one seemed to notice until a seemingly telekinetic force overturned Lily's drink. She sat there bemused as her geometrically patterned sleeve wicked up the sticky liqueur.

Giorgio fixed coldly on Bruce. "I told you not to drink too much." He spoke in Italian, his voice soft and pungent with control. Lily realized with surprise that she could understand the language.

"Why not," Bruce said, "since you're indulging yourself." The Italian words were flattened, wrung through his clenched jaw. He gripped the table edge and made an effort to focus his eyes on Giorgio. "I didn't come here to watch you with this cheap American whore." He lit a cigarette and tossed the match into the spilled amaretto, where it fizzled and emitted a feeble gasp of smoke.

Rhonda did not move, though she seemed to crouch into an unseen reserve. She stared across at Bruce and sang out in a fluent accent, "Carrrino—you simply can't be that much of a prude." She reached under the table toward Giorgio's waistband, keeping her eyes on Bruce. "Isn't it more like," she leaned toward Bruce while her fingers found a button, "you wish you were in my place?" Giorgio sat rigidly, glaring at Bruce. An erratic spotlight glare froze them all in grainy black and white, a tabloid photo.

Bruce turned his body a few degrees to face Rhonda. "What do you know?" he replied. His eyebrows arched above his half-lidded eyes as if he were about to sneeze or fall asleep. He deliberated. Finally he announced, "You don't even know," he rotated his head toward Lily, "that your prissy little roommate is a lesbian."

Lily lost track of language. What had he said? Did she understand correctly?

"What?" she said.

Giorgio said, "Stop, I don't understand." They had slipped into English.

"Your friend is being rude," Rhonda told him. She kept watching Bruce as she pulled at Giorgio's trousers. "You know what I think, Giorgio?" She began to fondle the wrinkled wool. "I think he's jealous." She poured her thickened voice in Giorgio's ear.

Giorgio made a truncated sound and pulled Rhonda's arm into his lap, clasping her hand. After a moment he signaled the waiter with a vague movement of his eyebrow. The man came with a white towel and mopped the table.

Lily stood up. The room spun a little as she turned and left.

Lily did not know how long she had been leaning against the wall outside of Green Time. The cool night air was a relief. She had found a darkened spot and stopped there, woozy and stunned. She wanted to recover before she decided what to do next.

When Rhonda appeared on the sidewalk, Lily was startled. Her heart began pounding and boomed in her head.

"You're still here," Rhonda said. "Are you going back to the room?"

Lily felt a vast gulf widening in her stomach. The trapdoor had opened and she had fallen through.

Rhonda continued, "You were right, he was awful. And so was his friend."

Lily began to feel sick. She did not want to think about it.

"They got in a big fight. It was ridiculous. I had to leave."

A cab reeled around the nearby piazza and shot off into a small alley-like street, then disappeared around a curve. Rhonda lit a cigarette and stood there exhaling defiantly.

She turned to Lily. "Anyway," she said, "is it true?" Her expression was concealed in shadow.

Lily leaned back against the wall and crossed her arms. "I don't know what you're talking about." Another cab burst toward them; Rhonda's face was lit up in the headlights. She could not contain her prurient curiosity.

"Lily. Come on. Tell," she persisted. "Are you?"

Lily saw their dark reflections in the plate glass window across the street. She was skinny and sharp next to Rhonda's expansive ebullience. She thought she could pop her like a balloon.

"It's true," Lily said. "I am unbelievably prim."

Contributors' Notes

MARY BRUNO ("Sweet Dreams")

Born in New Jersey, Mary Bruno once worked in a sleep lab. She's also had a long journalism, editing, and management career. Nowadays, she's a freelance writer who lives on Vashon Island, Washington.

"Over the years, I had sketched out snatches of what would become 'Sweet Dreams.' They were journal entries more or less, though a fleshed-out version of Elmer's attack on Walter was grist for a 1987 *Seattle Weekly* column. 'Sweet Dreams' became a story in 2002 when I spent five days at Hedgebrook, a writer's retreat on Whidbey Island, Washington.

The first draft introduced an ensemble of characters with the sleep lab as the default star. The response was mixed: Some people were uncomfortable with the descriptions of life as a lab animal; others seemed distracted by the details about sleep architecture and lab protocols. Nearly all the initial comments focused on point of view: Whose story is it, anyway?

It was Walter's story, though I'm not sure I knew that until I was asked.

I went back in and over the course of several weeks, gave Walter pale gray eyes, a wispy moustache and a diffident, tenderhearted manner. I inserted him and his point of view at the very beginning of the story and more consistently throughout. I tried to do a better job of connecting the story's scientific particulars to its characters and plot."

BEN GEBHARDT ("Birdhouses")

Ben Gebhardt (husband of Courtenay, below) is a mostly Seattle resident, raised in Hawaii. He was a construction worker during the workshop, is now a full-time grad student, and a couple of years as a broiler cook left an impression on him, too.

"My piece started in the third person, and as is my continual problem with first drafts, I perceived it contained everything I had felt about this character, Tom. At workshop, the resounding response was: 'Who is Tom, and why is he acting this way?' I went home and spoke everything I knew about Tom into a tape recorder. I compared that with my draft and saw that almost none of it showed up. I was surprised to find that many pages of the first draft amounted to woo-woo symbols acting as crutches for the missing character information. I did a complete rewrite of the story in the first person, and though it took months—squeezed in and around a construction schedule—I eventually came up with a much more powerful and intimate story."

COURTENAY GEBHARDT ("Noli Me Tangere")

Courtenay Gebhardt is a Eugene, Oregonian cum Seattleite who worked for several years as an editorial assistant with a famous online retail company. She gave birth to her first son in October 2002 (see husband Ben, above).

"One night, after Ben and I spent a day touring the art in Florence, we flopped down on our bed at the hostel and listened to our Walkman. When I closed my eyes, all I could see were those myriad pictures of Mary sadly holding Jesus and of Jesus crucified with blood pouring out of his side. The song we were listening to happened to be about death—how many random lives are lost in this 'bone grinding mill' each day— and it began with this image of a priest getting shot to death while he ate a hot dog. Call it plagiarism, but I knew I *had* to write the story of that man.

I began this piece after our first writing class. In the past I've only tried to write what I 'knew.' And always, writing was a teeth-pulling endeavor. This story wrote itself before I ever touched a keyboard. As I lay in bed awake at night, as I stood in the shower, as I drove in the car, the images and scenes just poured into me. Then I sat down one afternoon and it was done.

Critique helped with the parts that I suspected were fuzzy. The scene of Henri remembering France originally felt 'traveloguey,' as one reader put it, but I had let it slide because my attention was focused on another thread when I wrote it. Her calling it out helped me to take time (once again: in bed, at 2 a.m.) to press into the moment. What *was* Henri feeling when he thought about his childhood so long ago? And then grandmère appeared.

In class, later on, the question came up as to why I would choose Rome, medieval art, and an archbishop who's old and dying for my topic. Wasn't that beyond me, a 27-year-old American woman with only basic knowledge of art history? I'm still nagged by the suspicion that I got in over my head. Inside though, I can still *feel* the connection between the characters, the plot, and the 'point' of the story. I suppose learning to write is learning how to make your readers feel it with you."

MICHELLE GOODMAN ("THE HIVE")

Michelle Goodman has been a freelance writer and editor for ten years and has lived in Seattle for five years. Michelle's nonfiction writing has appeared in alternative weekly newspapers, in-flight magazines, and the anthology *Moment of Truth: Women's Funniest Romantic Catastrophes* (Seal Press, 2002). She's a native of Livingston, New Jersey.

"As an all-girls camp survivor, I've always wanted to write a story about the (potential) horrors of sleepaway camp. 'The Hive' began as a homework assignment for class. I wrote a scene about a girl who's so frustrated by her summer camp experience that she vandalizes the mess hall. This became the ending of draft one of 'The Hive.'

I wrote the full first draft of this story over a couple of days in March 2002. Feedback from the group was enormously helpful. Readers wanted to get inside Danielle's head more and understand her feelings and motivations. Jean's comment to think more *cinematically* was the suggestion that resonated the most with me.

I didn't return to the story till June. I pretty much scrapped the original version of the tale and made a detailed outline of a new draft. While trying to write from this outline, I panicked. The story had grown too complex, requiring too many characters and scenes. In September, when I got my head screwed on straight—thanks to Jean and Anne Lamott's *Bird by Bird*—I spent a week getting the second draft down. I tossed my notes and outline but knew they hadn't been for naught: By the time I sat down to write, I felt like I knew Danielle intimately. In the first draft of the story, Danielle was slinging insults at The Five every page or so. Fran was the one with the mild demeanor. Danielle sold out Fran, rather than the other way around. I love that the roles have since reversed.

Feedback on the second draft encouraged me to insert more lighthearted, quirky details into the story. Though I loved the story's darkness, most agreed it was too dismal. Jean's request to paint the art shack as more of a hippie sanctuary was crucial in helping me give the tale some additional levity. And I was thrilled there was actually a place for Joni Mitchell in my story."

JASON HERMAN ("Thaw")

Jason Herman recently left his position as a project manager for a major international software company to become a Ph.D. student. His first daughter was born soon after he completed this story. He's a native of Spokane, Washington.

"My first attempts at this story included scenes of Sneva being lonely at home, missing his daughter who had recently come to visit him for a few days. I drafted one scene in which Sneva takes a rotten pumpkin out to the garbage pile in his backyard and sees the boy, Jacob, working on his truck. The idea was supposed to be that Sneva sees that the boy is responsible, hard-working, and lonely like himself, so he asks the boy to watch his dog for the weekend, hoping that a relationship will develop out of the favor.

None of this, of course, makes for an engrossing read; it's all just setup for the actual story—which is about a boy's foolish mistake, an old man's weak attempt at being a savior, and a lie. However, in my first drafts I wasn't able to get to the actual story because I bored myself to death with rotten pumpkins and stale conversations between Sneva and Jacob about how to feed a dog.

Then, in one of our workshops, Jean suggested that if we were having trouble writing a story, we should try just writing the ending. I went home that week and drafted the story in the span of a few hours, thinking all the time that I would go back and write the beginning later. When the draft was finished, however, I realized that the ending was the story—all the rest was just material I needed in order to know my characters but that my reader didn't need at all.

Once the story was finished, it didn't go through much revision. I made a few changes here and there based on comments I received in workshop, but for the most part the story you see here is very reflective of the first draft. When I wrote the story I entered more deeply into these characters' emotions than I ever had with another story—and revising without again entering into that consciousness seemed artificial, awkward.

One last thing. Originally, Jacob's mistake was going to be spilling a bottle of the old man's expensive dog shampoo.

However, I came to the conclusion that a frozen dog is more interesting than a puddle of shampoo."

DEBORAH F. LAWRENCE
("WHY YOU HATE PINK")

Deborah F. Lawrence teaches art in the Graduate School of Arts and Social Sciences at Lesley University and has worked as an arts educator for many years. She has a sturdy exhibition record as a visual artist. She was born and educated in the suburbs of L.A. and lived in nine or ten different places around California before settling in Seattle.

"This piece was undertaken during Jean's writing workshop in early 2002. I wrote the first draft almost effortlessly, in approximately three sittings of perhaps three to five hours apiece.

The piece is autobiographical. I found it especially tricky to navigate the critique process, especially when turns of plot were called into question. But the general experience of group criticism and revision helped me to exercise flabby muscles of recollection and embodiment. It turned out I was able to amplify, inflate and collapse sensations and moments from history without compromising the integrity of my so-called treasured memoir. In response to comments from the beloved peanut gallery, I changed the person and tense a number of times, then—in response to other comments—I went back to the original second-person/present tense.

I didn't feel I contributed much to the literary discussion (I am more interested in a writer's psychological authenticity than in turns of phrase or textural description). But I loved the group critiques at first: all that stimulating, gratifying, flattering attention! Somewhere—perhaps between the fifth and sixth revision of a particular story of mine—I began to see how my neurotic needs to please both the group and Jean (the benevolent authority figure) were interfering with my voice. I don't really think of the creative process as a delicate thing. But the group critiques helped me discover there is a vulnerable little core to my original gesture that must not be adulterated."

ELIZABETH McCARTHY ("THE BULL'S-EYE")

Beth McCarthy was born in Calhoun, Georgia, grew up in Marion, Indiana, and became a nurse at the end of WWII in Washington, DC, performing mostly operating-room duties. She and her late husband, a surgeon, lived and raised their ten children on the beach in Kailua, Hawaii. She kept her nurse's license current until last year. These days, Beth volunteers at the Seattle Repertory Theatre and belongs to a writing group and a poetry group at The Women's University Club of Seattle. Her entire family, which numbers 46 now, is required to meet for three days every three years.

"This story grew out of a birthday party given by my son, a single parent, for his son. There were two main challenges: One, could I see beyond literal truth, and two, did I have faith and perseverance enough to work until it felt right?

What helped was the encouragement of readers who knew I would find the right answers. What helped was 'give me a little more here, a little less there,' or 'how about putting this description closer to the action?' In short, encouragement with thought-out suggestions made a difference.

It was never meant to be Granny's story. It was meant to be ET's, but it didn't turn out that way. At first, I grudgingly followed the pull of the story. But as I did I felt a flow. I developed a sincere respect for the little old lady who has lived it all, seen the worst and the best, yet makes no pretense and has no warp—well, except maybe a little against nosey neighbors."

LISA ORLICK ("The Messenger")

A native of Philadelphia, Lisa Orlick has been living in
Seattle for ten years. Over the past 20 years she has been an
urban planner, a researcher in desert architecture and energy
management, and an antipoverty program developer. Currently
she is a contract grant writer and a full-time parent.

"In a compilation of *The New York Times* front pages, I came
upon a piece describing the 1973 Maa'lot Massacre. I was drawn
to the description of children falling from the sky, the images
of grieving parents, and the description of the frustration Golda
Meir was said to have experienced. I was inspired to write about
displaced grief. I wanted to use the vivid descriptions of the
place—those juxtapositions of gardens with violence, memories
with shellshocked faces—as well as to show the mysterious way
rituals move us through pain and suffering.

'The Messenger' sat unfinished for three years. I was
unsatisfied with Aaron's internal voice, and his relationship with
Miriam was flat. Then, after the Sbarro Restaurant bombing in
2001, I was drawn back to the story. Early readers of that second
version seemed to think there was a sexual relationship between
Aliza and Aaron (mostly American readers felt this, not Israelis,
interestingly). So when I went back to the piece in 2002 for this
class, I felt I had to really open up Miriam's role and better develop
that relationship in order to give room for the core issue of the
piece, which is the presence of rituals in changing times.

Writing about the conflict within Israel was complicated. I
anticipated readers would come to this story with highly charged
notions of right and wrong and often with limited intimate
knowledge of what years of war have done to both Jews and
Arabs. I didn't want to lose the sacred landscape and the
humanity of my characters in an attempt to craft a politically
correct narrative. That said, it was very satisfying to find that
my story was enriched by the critique from this particular class.
The story had already spent most if its life in the past tense,
but new feedback helped me move it into the present tense,

into a single day of waiting. I became curious as to how Aaron would deliver his final message and what would happen at the end of this ritual's life."

LUCY POND ("DANCING WITH THE DEVIL")

Lucy Pond is a well-known astrologer and tarot reader in Seattle. She was born and raised in the Seattle area.

"This story has its roots in timed writing exercises written in a Seattle café over the course of a few months in 1998. I didn't know where I was going with it at the time but I enjoyed writing through the voice of a ten-year-old named Annie. At that time, I wanted to turn my timed writing exercises into a story but wasn't successful.

I spent most of 1997 and 1998 trying to write a screenplay around Annie at various ages, but wasn't able to keep the story simple enough.

In 2001, I worked on a story about a middle-aged woman overcoming a lifelong fear of doing crossword puzzles. The critiques I received called for more backstory. I probably turned that story in to Jean eight or nine times trying to create an authentic voice and clear narrative. As I dug deeper, I ultimately reconnected with the ten-year-old girl from early timed writing exercises. Annie transformed into Loretta, a girl ignored by her mother, a reclusive, inaccessible crossword ace.

It was never easy to write this story. But I kept at it because the story kept getting better and more focused. The title transmuted, as the story changed, from 'Crosswords' to 'The Day My Life Changed' to 'Dancing with the Devil.'

I see this piece as an early chapter of a book about Loretta and her family."

MINDY SCHABERG
("Wonder Woman and Spider-Man")

A former nonprofit employee, Mindy Schaberg currently works as a law clerk in a Seattle firm. She was born in Tacoma, Washington, and raised in Colorado Springs, Colorado.

"I wrote a skeletal version of this story for one of Jean's short-story assignments. It's based on a childhood memory, which I'd actually forgotten until I was wracking my brains for a short-story subject. And when I remembered it, I couldn't believe I'd forgotten it—it's so juicy, although I can't for the life of me remember what Darren's mother actually told my mother. (I asked my mom and she can't either.) Originally the story was mostly from Jill's point of view with mad veers into Darren's head, which was the first thing the group wanted me to fix. Another thing that surfaced immediately was a lack of information about Jill's motivation. Jean encouraged me to draw the rock vs. gem out as a metaphor. I did another draft with a single point of view (Jill's) to which people responded very kindly—though Julie was a staunch supporter of the original climactic foray into Darren's thoughts.

I put it away for a long period of time and tinkered sporadically here and there. When the group agreed to do this book project, Jean's red pen was uncapped with vengeance and she pushed for details, details, details, and still more about Jill. I worked very hard on it for about a week. In the group discussion, the timeframe—when things happened in the story—came up as an issue. I put away it again, and when I came back to it, I thought: This is terrible, the sense of time *is* all screwed up! You can't tell what happens when! And I pieced it together again. Then back to the group. Very positive feedback, with Courtney's suggestion this time that the adult voices were a little bland and to rework that. Back for a little more tweaking and reworking and here we are. I have never put so much time into 3,200 words, but I'm amazed at the result."

JULIE SCHICKLING ("GREEN TIME")

Julie Schickling works in the engineering world, using computers to draw buildings, roads, and other trappings of civilization. She was born in Merced, California and spent her early years moving all over the country. When she was in the eighth grade her family arrived in Seattle, where she has remained.

"I wrote the beginning of 'Green Time' for a class on 'Writing about Place' that I took at the Richard Hugo House [Literary Center]. At that point, the story ended right after Rhonda introduced Lily to Giorgio (originally Tomasso) and he went off to get the drinks. I got the basic idea for the rest of it about a year later during a 2001 class with Jean when I decided to take a break from a novel-length work. I wrote most of the rest of 'Green Time' in an intense burst for this 2002 class.

In general, class feedback was encouraging; most of the comments asked for details . . . of how Lily and Rhonda met, of how they related, for more about Giorgio. There was a memorable comment from Courtenay about the confrontational scene at the table; she said she wanted to see the 'train wreck.' The two main problems I worked out in the first revision were sketching Lily and Rhonda's history and showing the 'train wreck.' After that I concentrated on adding more description, trying to even out the tone, and developing the ending. One challenge has been having the time to get the distance I need to be able to see the story a little more objectively without putting off work on it indefinitely. Also, after getting comments that were directly opposite each other, I realized (of course, I already knew) that ultimately *I* have to decide what works; it's impossible to please everyone all the time."

SUNNY SPEIDEL ("MRS. MIM'S HELP")

Sunny Speidel has worked as a welder and a writer for a Seattle visitors' publication. In her current day job, she serves

as president (and intermittent guide) of Seattle's
Underground Tour, a historic walking tour of Seattle's Pioneer
Square. She was born and raised in Seattle.

"In one way, this story popped out fully formed. I'd just
returned from a long stay in Jamaica, feeling bothered as usual
by the poverty and inequality in most of the world. This story
became a chance to speak of it.

On the other hand, this story contained rather serious
structural flaws. It's the first piece of fiction I've written in my
adult life, and I'd neglected to include things like an
introduction to the characters and an ending.

Many readers in class charitably offered that they thought
the story was actually a chapter in a novel, and that the crucial
missing elements must lay elsewhere, invisible to their eyes.
Nonetheless, I gleaned from them what it was I needed to do
to the story.

It was just one manifestation of what it feels like to have a
roomful of people rooting for you as you learn something of
the craft of writing. Because of Jean and the remarkable people
in this class, I learned a lot in a very short time. None of it came
the way I thought it would, like the discipline of learning the
multiplication tables. Instead it came in strange little intuitive
leaps. I like that part the best."

ERIKA TESCHKE ("DISTINCT AND DIFFERENT")

A native of Dallas, Erika Teschke is now a legal supervisor
at a firm in Seattle. She has also worked as a race-horse groom.

"I started 'Distinct and Different' because the pressure
was on, class deadline was the next day, and I had to have
something to turn in. I spent at least an hour messing
around with a few small paragraphs and tiny beginnings I
had written some weeks and years before. Stuff I had really
liked and wanted to go somewhere. None of it worked and
it was getting late. So I cussed and started fresh. That was
late March 2002.

Since then I have pounded through ten revisions. I spent a lot of time thinking about my characters, usually while waiting for the bus or walking to work. Placing them out in the world and trying to get a sense of who they were. The writing part was more work. I am not a very fast writer and I have a show-and-tell problem, which really slowed things up once I had the plot established. But I always had a sense the story was going to involve a Sara Lee and a fresh-faced, Ivy League do-gooder so my plot came out quite easily. With just a few natural transgressions and progressions, the plot still exists as it did in the first version.

Feedback in class really helped me focus on areas that I knew were problematic, like the mother. I wanted her to infiltrate the reader's mind, but not too much. I wanted her to be evil, believable, and pitiful. One of my best friends growing up had a mother like her and although I knew she existed, I had trouble making her come alive in a real way for the readers. Always afraid of making her too much of a Cruella De Vil type, I tended not to give her enough life. Instead she became stereotypic, since the few descriptive tidbits I gave her weren't enough to make her distinct. Courtenay's tireless comments on version seven finally gave me the insight I needed. She wrote 'Your story deals directly w/ life's complexity; it seems like your characters could benefit from a dose of it.' Duh! I stopped being afraid of giving them loose ends at that point. Further class reactions helped me to recognize when I had hit just the right detail. When the matching Hermès belt and shoes made Michelle roll her eyes in sympathy, I knew I was getting close."

GLORIA UPPER ("DICKEYFISH")

Gloria Upper spent 11 years as a graphic artist at University of Washington Press and elsewhere, designing catalogs, advertising, books, and book jackets. She's also been an editor, a secretary, a ski instructor, a playwright, and the owner of a fishing boat and an antique shop. Gloria is a fourth-generation Seattleite. She married young during WWII and has three middle-aged children and five grandchildren. She presently volunteers as a drawing teacher at Lifetime Learning Center in Seattle.

"The story of 'Dickeyfish' is based on a disturbing and mysterious memory that returned to haunt me a couple of years ago. I felt impelled to write about this remote little girl (who was me) and discover why she killed her fish. The first version was written in a Friday Harbor writer's workshop, won first prize at the San Juan County Fair Writers' Corner, and then was put aside.

Jean's writing group seemed a perfect and safe venue for further exploration and development of the piece. I was amazed at the additional memories and discoveries, both real and imaginary, that kept coming during the process, and which related and added to the story.

Although the story takes place in the 1930s during the Depression, long before most of my workshop classmates were born, I found their questions and comments—particularly ones about the girl's motivation—helped me to further clarify the story. Some classmates understood the girl's actions immediately and others were more persuaded when I added details that showed the buildup of pressure upon her from the mother and grandmother. Everyone liked the story. Their insights and sympathy for the character, and encouraging and positive feedback, aided me in my progress.

The title was ultimately changed from 'The Demise of Dickeyfish' to just 'Dickeyfish' as some in the group felt the original was too casual or light. One writer thought that the story should be in third person rather than first person, but the majority of the group liked the first-person version. I like to combine fact and fiction and hope the story will become one of a group of semi-autobiographical short pieces that I am working on."

G